Annie Henry

and the
Secret Mission

★ ★ ★ ★ ★ ★ ★ ★ ★ ★ ★ ★ ★ ★ ★ ★
ADVENTURES OF THE AMERICAN REVOLUTION
★ ★ ★ ★ ★ ★ ★ ★ ★ ★ ★ ★ ★ ★ ★ ★

Annie Henry

and the
Secret Mission

Susan Olasky

CROSSWAY BOOKS • WHEATON, ILLINOIS
A DIVISION OF GOOD NEWS PUBLISHERS

Annie Henry and the Secret Mission

Copyright © 1995 by Susan Olasky

Published by Crossway Books
        a division of Good News Publishers
        1300 Crescent Street
        Wheaton, Illinois 60187

Cover illustration: Tom LaPadula

Art Direction/Design: Mark Schramm

First printing, 1995

Printed in the United States of America

Library of Congress Cataloging-in-Publication Data
Olasky, Susan.
    Annie Henry and the secret mission / Susan Olasky.
        p.   cm.—(Adventures of the American Revolution).
    Summary: Patriot Patrick Henry's ten-year-old daughter Annie helps save the wheat crop on their Virginia plantation from fire and her father from a Tory spy in Richmond.
    [1. Henry, Patrick, 1736-1799—Fiction. 2. Virginia—Fiction.
3. Courage—Fiction. 4. Fathers and Daughters—Fiction.] I. Title.
II. Series.
PZ7.0425An 1995   [Fic]—dc20   94-38671
ISBN 0-89107-830-4

03		02		01		00		99		98		97		96		95
15	14	13	12	11	10	9	8	7	6	5	4	3	2	1

For
Marvin

CONTENTS

I

FIRE!

ANNIE HENRY STOOD AT THE SECOND FLOOR WINDOW making faces at the men working in the fields below. They couldn't see her, of course, but it gave her satisfaction just the same. Ten minutes earlier she had been outside watching the men from close-up. She was full of curiosity about the harvest as she darted back and forth between the mowers with the big scythes and the reapers with their smaller sickles.

Then, her almost brother-in-law, John Fontaine, had grown annoyed and ordered her into the house. "Annie, you're in the way," he said. "Go inside and stay where you belong. We've got a harvest to bring in before the rain."

As she remembered his words, her face grew hot. He hadn't even trusted her to go alone to the house but had taken her by the hand and led her there, a quarter of a mile. Annie imagined that she had heard the men laugh as she was led away in disgrace.

Now she stood at the window, a small, ten-year-old, dark-haired girl silhouetted against the glass. Together with her little sister Elizabeth, she gazed out at the flurry of activity below.

It was hard for Annie to stay angry. She knew John Fontaine was right, and from the window she could see a storm coming.

Annie called to her sister who was four years younger. "Elizabeth, look at all those men. Doesn't it look like they are racing the storm?" She showed off the knowledge she had recently obtained. "See the scythe? They use it to cut the wheat. See that other man behind? He bundles the wheat into sheaves."

"Why do they work so fast?" Elizabeth asked.

"Because there's a storm coming," Annie replied. "If we don't get the wheat cut and covered, it will be lost. Look at the clouds over there." She pointed in the distance where a thin line of black clouds lined the horizon.

Elizabeth turned back to her dolls, but Annie continued to watch out the window. On a clear day you could see the mountains near Charlottesville, more than sixty miles away. But not today. As Annie watched, the wind kicked up. In the distance, lightning darted from a cloud.

Her attention turned from the sky back to the men in the field. Other men followed the mowers whose job it was to stack the sheaves into shocks. Eight sheaves stood up on end, and two were laid across the top like a roof so that rain couldn't damage the grain. Soon, shocks of wheat looking like little houses dotted the field. The men, aware of the advancing storm, worked faster and faster as they struggled to cut and sheave the last field.

Although each man did something different—the mower cut the grain, the gripper bundled it, and a third man tied it—they worked together as one, Annie thought. Each man knew his job and did it quickly. They dropped those sheaves and went on while other men came behind and stacked them. Up and down the field they worked until nothing but the edges were left uncut. Annie knew that poor people could come and glean at the edges of the field and get whatever grain remained.

"They're going to finish, Elizabeth," Annie said with a laugh. "They beat the storm."

The girls looked up at the sky. The clouds were closer, but the rain had not started and the men were finished. She felt a rush of satisfaction. Her father, Patrick Henry, would be glad. As soon as he returned home to his plantation, there would be a celebration.

A flash in the distant sky caught Annie's attention. More lightning, she thought, but it doesn't matter now. The harvest is done. Now all we have to do is thresh the wheat, and that can wait. She turned her attention to the room in which she stood.

It was a long room that stretched the length of the house. Usually it served as a playroom for the younger Henry children. But on special occasions it would be transformed into a ballroom. That's where the party would be tomorrow when her father returned.

Returning to the window, a look of concern creased her brow. In the distance she thought she saw a fine line of smoke. "Elizabeth, come here," she ordered.

Elizabeth rushed to the window. "Do you see anything out there?" Annie asked as she pointed.

"What do you mean?" Elizabeth responded, peering out the window.

"Do you see smoke?" Annie asked.

Elizabeth shook her head. "I don't see it," she said and went back to her dolls.

But Annie stayed at the window. She wasn't sure she had seen anything. Now it just looked like clouds.

Another bolt of lightning darted down from the clouds, and she thought she saw another stream of smoke. But when she looked again, what she had thought was smoke had blended so perfectly with the storm clouds that she wasn't sure.

"What if I go down there and tell them there's a fire, and I'm wrong?" she wondered out loud. "John Fontaine would be furious."

Annie waited with indecision. The wind picked up. The branch of a walnut tree scraped the window. She could hear the heavy limbs moan with the wind. A third bolt of lightning lit up the sky, and Annie saw more smoke.

"I know it's fire," she said to Elizabeth. "I've got to warn them. It has been so hot and dry this summer, the stubble in the fields could easily catch on fire."

Elizabeth joined Annie once more at the window. "Wouldn't they smell it?" her little sister asked.

Annie shook her head. "I think it's still too far away."

She tugged at the heavy window but it wouldn't budge. "Help me open this window," Annie said impatiently.

The two small girls struggled with the window but could only move it an inch. Annie knew it was useless to pound on the glass. The men were much too far to hear.

"I'll go down and warn them," Annie told Elizabeth. "Stay here and watch the fields. Surely you see the smoke now."

Elizabeth nodded. There were three distinct trails of black smoke rising to meet the lighter gray storm clouds.

"You have to let us know if the smoke is coming closer," Annie said. "We won't be able to see it from the ground. You'll have to signal." Looking around for something to use as a flag, she finally grabbed the red sash from her dress. "If the fire comes closer to the wheat fields you must hang this sash out the window. I'll watch for the sign, and I'll be able to tell the men." Annie grabbed her sister by the shoulders and said fiercely, "You have to pay attention, Elizabeth. It's important. Can you do it?"

Elizabeth nodded. Her eyes were wide as she watched the little tails of smoke get bigger and begin to merge as the fire spread. Annie ran down the stairs and out the door. The wind caught up her long skirts and twisted them about her legs, but she didn't stop. She yelled as she ran, but the men were still too far away to hear. Her side ached, but she kept going. Finally, breathless, she reached the harvesters, grabbed the arm of the closest man, and said, "Fire," while pointing across the fields.

The reaction was immediate. Men jumped up from the ground where they had been drinking water and eating cornbread. Annie watched John Fontaine bark orders. Several men ran to the barn for horses. Minutes later a wagon hooked to a team of oxen appeared, loaded with shovels, four large water barrels, and leather buckets. A few men climbed on while others had already started running across the field. John Fontaine grabbed one of the waiting horses and galloped off in the direction of the fire.

No one paid attention to Annie who suddenly remembered Elizabeth waiting at the window. Looking over, she saw the red sash hanging out. "The fire is coming this way," she yelled fearfully. "My sister is watching it from the window."

A farmer shouted the news to the men on the hay

wagon. In the confusion, no one noticed Annie climb onto the wagon. She could smell the smoke now. Little pieces of ash floated from the sky as the wind gusted. "Oh, Lord," she prayed. "Let it rain now. Let it rain."

It was hard traveling across the field because of all the ridges and furrows. Up a ridge the wagon would go, then down a furrow, until Annie felt she would get sick to her stomach. When the wagon finally found a road through the field, travel was easier. But it still took a long time for the wagon to get out to the fire.

The closer the wagon drew, the hotter the air. Annie found it hard to breathe. Her eyes watered and her throat burned. She could see orange flames blazing up from the dry stubble and wheat shocks. The fire didn't care whether it consumed the wheat or the chaff. All of it was burning.

Annie shielded her face with the wide sleeve of her dress. The wagon stopped and the men jumped out, joining the men who were already in the field. They were beating the flames in a fruitless attempt to put them out. When the wagon arrived they grabbed shovels and began digging a trench to contain the fire. But the wind was an enemy. Gusts easily carried the burning wheat across the trenches like little torches that sent the dry stubble up in flames.

The men had to retreat before the blazing fire. Several moved the wagon back to get it out of danger. They feared the fire would surround them, leaving them no way of escape.

Others formed a bucket brigade to move the water from the barrel on the wagon to the fire. One man filled the bucket and passed it down the chain until the man on the end emptied it. Then the empty buckets were passed back. Back and forth went the buckets until the water from the barrel was all gone.

As they dampened the blaze in one place, it sprung up somewhere else, but the men kept working. Acrid smoke filled the air, making Annie cough until she felt she would faint. A farmer shoved a wet rag at her and told her to tie it across her mouth. Then he handed her a bucket and told her to work.

Annie worked side-by-side with the men until she was worn out. Then she worked some more. When the rag dried out, she dipped it in the water and tied it back on. Still she labored.

Finally, they had used all the water in all the barrels. They had dug the trenches. There was nothing more to do. And the fire still burned. All around, as far as Annie could see, hay shocks had been consumed. She felt an overwhelming sadness. They had tried desperately to save the harvest, and they hadn't been able to do it.

A bolt of lightning followed immediately by a clap of thunder lit up the field. More lightning meant more fire, but Annie was too tired to care. She walked sadly to the wagon where the men were wearily taking off their gloves. No one spoke a word. Just then, she felt something that gave her a spark of hope. At first Annie wasn't sure: maybe it was just a splash from a water bucket or a piece of ash. But then, as if heaven had opened, the rain began to fall. It fell in a downpour, and the raging fires were quickly extinguished.

A cry went up from the farmers. It sounded unlike any cry Annie had ever heard: a crazy, yelping, howling cry of joy—and Annie found herself yelping along with the men.

John Fontaine did not join the others in their celebration. Annie glanced at him, a lone figure with his head bowed and his knees on the ground giving thanks to God. Then he roused himself and directed the men. Since the rain had turned the field into mud, John ordered several men to unhitch the oxen and walk them back to the barn.

As he looked around, he noticed Annie for the first time. "How did you get out here?" he demanded. But before she could speak, he went on, "We'll talk later. You ride back with me. Patsy will be worried sick."

John helped Annie onto the horse, then swung up behind her. Before they rode off, he turned to the wet and tired men in the fields. "Thank you," he said to them. "You helped."

Annie's big sister Patsy was waiting on the steps when they rode up. She rushed down the stairs and looked anxiously from John to Annie. "Are you hurt? Annie, what happened to you? What about Father's wheat?" The questions tumbled out so fast that neither John nor Annie had time to answer.

John smiled and took Patsy's hand. "We're all fine. We probably lost a field. I'll know better tomorrow. But thank God for Annie's warning. We were able to slow down the spread of the fire until the rain came."

The three stood under the porch roof for a minute, thinking about the near disaster. Then Patsy said, "You're soaked, Annie. And you're covered with soot. Go inside."

After Annie ran into the house, Patsy turned and asked John, "What were you thinking to let a little girl go out to fight a fire?" Patsy's voice broke.

"I'm sorry, Patsy. It was my fault. I did not see her get on the wagon. But God preserved her."

She nodded. "I know I shouldn't worry so much, John. But I feel so responsible. With Mama ill and Father away, the burden falls on me. Annie takes so many unnecessary risks. Father must do something."

"He will, Patsy. But let your father do it. She needs a mother's gentle touch—and her mother can't give it."

2

SCOTCHTOWN

ANNIE LOVED EVERY FOOT OF SCOTCHTOWN, THE plantation house she lived in with her family. Sitting on a hill in the fertile farmland of central Virginia, the house was impressive. It was a two story white clapboard structure with eight large and eight small windows across the front. Large stone stairs led to the front door which opened onto a long hallway that cut the house in two. Annie sometimes imagined that she could open the doors at both ends of that hallway and ride a pony right through the house.

On either side of that hallway were four rooms, each one heated by a huge corner fireplace. The second story was a single room, sometimes used for large parties, but usually reserved as a nursery for Elizabeth and Edward.

But Scotchtown was more than a house. It was a little village. At the back of the house were separate buildings: her father Patrick Henry's office, the kitchen, bedrooms for her brothers William and John, and one for the children's tutor, Richard Dabney. There was also a dry well—a hole more than twenty feet in the ground that stayed constantly cool. In it was stored milk, butter, and cheese so they would not spoil.

Further away from the house was a dairy, a blacksmith shop, a stable, and many sheds for farm implements. And further still were the small cottages where thirty slaves lived.

Patrick Henry owned 1000 acres, but only 400 were cleared and planted. The rest was woodland and meadow. Scotchtown was a wonderful place for the six Henry children to live. Patsy, at seventeen, was the oldest. Then came William, fifteen, John, thirteen, Annie, who was ten, Elizabeth, five, and the baby, Edward, who was three.

Annie Henry had explored much of the farm. That's because Patrick Henry thought his children should spend much of their time outside in the woods, running free. Annie agreed with her father. She was a reluctant pupil, and her morning lessons with the tutor were often painful.

But today there were no lessons. Annie whistled with delight as she jumped out of bed. Today, Father was coming home. And better still, it was the day for the harvest party—and the farm buzzed with activity.

Patrick Henry had been a busy man in the year of

1774. He had spent weeks in Richmond and Williamsburg on business, sometimes attending meetings of the House of Burgesses—Virginia's legislature where laws were made. Lately, he had been even busier. Tensions had increased between the colonies and the king, and Patrick Henry was a spokesman for many Virginians.

That meant that Annie's father was rarely home. His law practice suffered, and his family missed him. Annie thought she missed him the most.

Standing in front of the mirror, she tried to get her stubborn brown hair to cooperate. It was important that she look just right for her father's return. But her wiry hair had ideas of its own. So she pulled it back in a simple ponytail at the back of her neck and tied it with a ribbon. It would have to do.

Annie wore a dress of white cotton like most girls her age. Its full skirts reached the floor, and its wide, ruffled sleeves made good hiding places for books or cookies or pebbles found on her walks. She wore soft leather boots because Patsy insisted. But Annie knew, as did Patsy, that as soon as she ran outside, the boots would come off so that she could run barefoot.

When Annie was satisfied, she went outdoors. The air was heavy after the evening's rain, and it still smelled like wet, burnt wheat. But the rain had washed away the smoke, so she could see a long way. One whole part of the field was charred. The shocks were black; the wheat was ruined.

Her stomach rumbled. She sniffed the air for a hint of bacon or biscuits and was rewarded by inviting smells. Just then, she heard the bell for breakfast. Annie went around the side of the house to a small door. She dashed up the stairs and into the family dining room. Patsy looked up when her sister entered the room. "Gracious, Annie, there's no need to be running in and out of the servants' entrance. You could enter the room like a lady. Come and eat. I don't think I can hold off John and William. They look to be starving."

The two young men, Annie's big brothers, laughed. William shared his father's prominent nose and deep-set eyes, but John, like Annie, resembled their mother, and like Annie, he was plagued with curly hair and freckles. Neither boy showed any of Patrick Henry's interest in learning. When they could escape the schoolmaster, they went hunting and fishing with friends from neighboring farms. Of course, the boys bragged, their father had been a lazy student also, but Patsy didn't like to hear about that.

Holding her nose, Annie came to the table. "You boys smell like smoke," she said with disgust. "Didn't you bathe?"

"Bathe? Why we had baths last week. You know it isn't healthful to bathe too often," William said as he pretended to grab the last of the biscuits.

Annie slipped into the seat next to him and plunked the biscuit onto her own plate. "I took a bath and I suggest you do too. Being next to you is like being in the fire all over again."

"Were you scared, Annie?" John asked.

She nodded. "I didn't know it would be so big and out of control. My arms are stiff from those water buckets. But let's not talk about it. Father is coming home. I'm so excited I don't know if I can eat," she said as she buttered and jellied another piece of bread and put it into her mouth.

"Annie, I don't think there's ever been a moment when you couldn't eat," John laughed. "You're going to become big and fat one of these days."

Patsy laughed, "If I ate like Annie I'd likely grow as big as a barn. But Annie doesn't sit still long enough. She runs around more than you. I wouldn't be surprised if Annie couldn't outrun you and outfish you, John Patrick."

"And if you got as big as a barn it doesn't seem likely that cousin John Fontaine would be wanting to marry you, does it?" asked William slyly.

Blushing, Patsy stared at her plate while she chewed the last bite of sausage. Annie giggled and kicked William under the table.

"Who's going to meet Father?" Annie asked when she stopped giggling. "I can't decide whether to wait for him or to watch the preparations for the party. I love harvest time."

"Especially this one. Can you imagine if we lost all the wheat—and Father away?" William asked. "I'm glad we don't have to tell him bad news like that. Now we can celebrate."

Nodding in agreement, Patsy said with some pride, "I'm glad John Fontaine was here to take control. Father left the farm in good hands."

John interrupted. "But it was Annie who deserves the credit. She saw the fire and warned us. If she hadn't, the fire would have spread faster. We would have lost much more."

Annie blushed and smiled gratefully at John. It was nice to be recognized. She thought happily of the fact that Father would surely be told of her role in saving the wheat.

Forcing a smile, Patsy added, "Annie also acted foolishly. She should not have been out riding on a hay wagon in the middle of a fire. She risked her own life and the lives of others."

Annie's eyes welled up. She knew that Patsy was right, but before she could speak John said, "That's silly, Patsy. Annie didn't get in anyone's way. I was there, and I know what I'm talking about. In fact, she emptied buckets and worked like any of the men."

"Hush! John Patrick," Patsy said sharply. "I know

where Annie belongs, and it isn't in a hay wagon in the middle of a fire. And I have to say what's right . . . . That's my job, even if you don't understand. How would we explain to Father if Annie had been injured? Would you be responsible? No, I would be."

While Patsy spoke the other children looked around uncomfortably, and the playful teasing of just a few minutes ago disappeared.

Excusing himself from the table, William grabbed his rifle from the rack over the fireplace and marched outside. John grabbed his hat and followed. That left only Annie and her older sister. Patsy rose but not before Annie saw the tear slip down her sister's cheek.

Annie looked around the empty room. Minutes before it had been filled with laughter. "I'm sorry, Patsy," she said. "I didn't mean to worry you."

Patsy hugged her tight. "I know you didn't. But you have to learn to think."

Excusing herself, Annie went outside. She walked out back to a small, fenced enclosure where her chickens pecked at the still wet ground. "You'll have a tasty meal of crickets and grubs after that rain," she said as she scattered dried corn for the hens. Her father had bought her a rooster and three hens a year ago. Raising chickens was a good activity for a young girl, he said. Now she had ten hens which she tended faithfully every morning. She gathered the eggs in her basket and took them to the kitchen where she emptied them into a crockery bowl before returning the basket to the coop.

"I guess I'll go out to the road," she said. "Perhaps Father will come early. I'm too excited about the party to stay here smelling all that food cooking."

She took off her boots, leaving them on the porch, and set off toward the road. The ground was wet, and Annie's feet were soon muddy. She looked unhappily at the hem of her once white dress.

The road was not paved. It was nothing more than wagon ruts thick with mud after the night's rain. Hitching up her dress, she stepped into the cool mud. It squeezed between her toes. Then she put one muddy foot in a puddle and swirled it until the mud floated off.

Walking a little further, she came to a dry spot under a hickory nut tree where she filled her pockets with green nuts that had fallen during the storm. For the next half hour, Annie amused herself by tossing hickory nuts to the squirrels who chattered noisily in the trees around her. The boldest ones scampered nervously after the nuts. Annie so successfully distracted herself that she didn't notice the dust trails down the pike. But she heard a voice calling her name. She jumped up—and there, about twenty yards down the road, was her father, Patrick Henry.

He galloped to her, reached down, and swung Annie up off her feet in one fluid motion.

"So only little Annie came to watch for me," he said.

She laughed. Her face glowed with pleasure. "I couldn't just sit in the house and wait. I had to come see."

Her father continued to hold her close. "I thought I might find you here," he said with a smile. "I brought a treat back for the child who waited." Pulling a maple sugar candy out of his pocket, he handed it to his daughter.

"Here. Let's ride back," he said, putting her in front of him on his big black horse and urging the horse toward the house.

"Is the harvest finished?" he asked as he looked about the fields.

"They finished the wheat yesterday, before the rain," Annie said.

"Then I guess we'll have a celebration—or did you celebrate without me?"

"We didn't celebrate. We almost lost everything in a fire. It started by lightning. But John Fontaine and the men fought it—and I think they saved a good deal of the wheat," his young daughter explained.

Patrick Henry's face clouded. "That wheat means everything to us since we don't grow tobacco. I'll ride out with John later. But no more bad news," he said. "Tell me about the harvest party."

"You mean we can still celebrate?" Annie asked. "Will you play the violin?"

"Tonight?" he said while yawning. "Oh, I'm much too tired. I must go to bed early tonight, child."

"But you can't," Annie protested. "You have to . . . ." She turned in the saddle to look at him and saw a twinkle in his deep-set eyes.

"Oh, Father. You're just kidding. I knew you'd play the fiddle. You always do."

Patrick Henry laughed.

It was a perfect July night. Stars hung low in the sky. The crickets chirped, and fireflies flashed in the dark. Annie sat on the porch waiting for the guests to arrive. She wore a green silk party dress with tiny white flowers and lace. Patsy had put her hair up with green ribbons, and she wore delicate leather slippers on her feet. Annie felt more like a princess than a little girl from Virginia.

Soon the wagons and carriages arrived filling up the front lawn. Annie curtsied to the ladies and delivered them to Patsy who waited in the ladies' parlor. The men she led to her father's study.

The men looked like strangers tonight. They had taken off their farming clothes and put on silk knee breeches and hip coats. Their wigs were powdered, and their leather shoes shined.

After receiving the guests, she ran upstairs. The servants were still arranging the tables with food and flowers, but they paid no attention to young Annie. She grabbed a handful of mints from a bowl and inspected the other food. There was cider and punch, ham and beef, pies and cakes, and enough food to feed a small army.

Soon Annie heard footsteps on the stairs, and the guests began entering. The large room quickly filled with Patrick Henry's friends and neighbors who danced while the children's tutor played the harpsichord. Then Annie's father grabbed his violin and began to play. The dancing switched from the sedate minuet to lively Scottish reels, and Annie joined the dancers.

Finally, her father called for everyone's attention. "It is wonderful to be home," he began, "in the heart of my family. I thank God for them and for my safe travel. But we must also give thanks for the abundant harvest He has given us. And thank you who fought the fires . . . ." Patrick Henry's voice caught, but then he continued, "Thank God none of you was injured, and the grain was saved." He raised his goblet in a toast, catching Annie's eye and winking.

Everyone clapped and the music resumed. Although Annie tried to stay awake until the guests left, she couldn't. She woke up briefly to find herself in bed, her father leaning over her and saying tenderly, "Sleep well, little one, sleep well." Annie smiled and drifted back to sleep.

3

THE ACCIDENTAL SWIM

BY OCTOBER, THE HARVEST PARTY WAS ONLY A MEMORY. Patrick Henry had stayed home for three weeks before leaving again. This time he went to Philadelphia where he would stay two months. He was representing Virginia at the Continental Congress where he and other important men would discuss what they should do about their disagreement with Great Britain.

Annie missed her father desperately. The fall days reminded her how long he'd been gone. The trees were dropping their leaves. Apples were ripening. The cider presses were running, and the hogs were being butchered.

She wandered out in the pasture watching the men plant wheat seed. They walked up and down the ridges in the field, scattering the seed by the handful. Annie felt at loose ends. Elizabeth was sick with a fever and had to stay in bed. Patsy was busy running the house and didn't have time for Annie. And the boys were out hunting. That left Annie with nothing to do.

Without planning, she found herself by the banks of a little creek that crossed one of the pastures. It was a favorite place for the boys to fish, but Annie hadn't brought a fishing pole. She walked along the bank until she came to a spot where the roots of a towering willow tree jutted into the water and formed, with leaves and twigs and other debris, a dam. The water was deep, and Annie could see at the bottom a big, gray fish that was just out of reach. The fish was playing hide-and-seek with her, swimming out in the open and then darting back under the bank of the creek where the shadows made it hard for her to see.

The day was warm for October, but the water was cold. Annie set one bare foot gingerly on a rock about a foot from shore. She planted her other foot firmly on the creek bank. The fish darted into the shadow. Annie thought for a minute. Maybe she could catch the fish the way the Indians did. Uncle William Christian was always full of Indian stories, and Annie loved to hear them.

She hopped over to the other side of the creek where she found a stick about five feet long and an quarter inch in diameter. She rubbed the end of it back and forth on a rock until a point emerged. Annie kept rubbing until the stick looked sharp. She tested it on her finger and winced as it pricked. Finally satisfied, she thought, "Now I'll get a fish."

Annie resumed her position of one foot on the rock in the creek and the other firmly on the creek bank. She waited. Then carefully leaning over, she aimed her sharpened stick at the fish. She held that position for a moment before plunging the stick into the water. The fish swam easily out of reach of the makeshift spear.

She tried several more times before giving up, tossing her spear into the stream with disgust. As she began to climb back to shore, her foot slipped on a slimy, algae-covered rock. Annie twisted in a vain attempt to keep her balance before tumbling into cold water up to her chest. She tried to stand, but her long skirts were heavy with water.

"Ugh," she groaned, dragging herself to the bank. "Now I'm in trouble." Barely had those words left her mouth when she heard the sound of laughter from the other side of the creek. She swung around in time to see a tall, middle-aged woman, dressed in a plain dress with a black calash—a hood-like hat—on her head.

Crawling onto the bank Annie began to wring water out of her skirts. The woman called out apologetically, "Please forgive me. You looked like you were having such a good time, and then you tumbled . . . and those silly skirts. I am sorry. How rude of me to laugh."

The woman talked as she crossed the creek, walking carefully across on stepping stones until she stood at Annie's side. She held out a woolen cloak. "Please take my coat. You'll catch your death of pneumonia."

Shaking her head, Annie replied, "I couldn't. Look at me." Her cotton dress had a mud streak up the back. Rivulets of water continued to stream from the heavy folds of fabric that clung to her legs and arms. A sudden breeze raised goosebumps on Annie's arms and sent dry leaves scudding across the fields.

"Oh, bother," the woman said. "Of course you'll take it. It can always be cleaned."

Annie hesitated, then gratefully wrapped the cloak around her.

"I'm Mrs. Thacker, a neighbor down the way," the woman said. "We've just bought the farm over there." She pointed out over the fields.

Annie smiled, "I'm Annie Henry. I live up in Scotchtown," she said pointing to the large house behind her.

"I was coming to Scotchtown," Mrs. Thacker said. "Could we walk together?"

The wet young girl nodded and the two set off. They were still about 100 yards from the house when Annie apologized, "I'll have to run ahead. My sister Patsy will spit coals when she sees my dress ruined. It's not the first one this week.

"Surely Patsy has tried spear fishing before," Mrs. Thacker said. "She probably wouldn't begrudge you a little fun."

"Oh, not Patsy. Patsy doesn't know the meaning of

fun. Or maybe she's just too old to have fun," Annie said, then caught herself with embarrassment. "Not that old people . . . I mean . . . . Oh, you know."

She bit her lip with regret.

Mrs. Thacker laughed. "Even old people like me have fun, Annie. But we also have responsibilities. It takes a while to figure out how to balance the two. Maybe that's what Patsy is figuring out."

"I guess," said Annie grudgingly. "But she'll be angry just the same. I'd rather not give her reason to be unhappy with me. After all, I meant no harm."

"Of course you didn't. You run ahead. I can find my way to the door," Mrs. Thacker said. She waved as Annie ran, dragging the oversized cloak in the dirt. "Oh well," the woman sighed, "nothing that a little soap and water can't get out."

Annie changed, putting the wet dress in the hamper with the other soiled clothes. She hung Mrs. Thacker's cloak in the wardrobe and then looked for Patsy in the ladies' parlor.

"Where is Mrs. Thacker?" Annie asked.

"She is visiting Mama," Patsy answered.

"Could I visit Mama?" Annie asked wistfully.

Patsy shook her head sadly. "Maybe when Father gets home, Annie." Patsy held a letter in her hand and smiled. "And he is coming home. This letter is dated eight days ago. He could be here anytime." Patsy's face lit up with a smile as Annie realized suddenly how tired her sister looked.

Returning the smile, Annie said, "You look pretty when you're happy, Patsy. I guess you've been working too hard."

Her older sister nodded. "I guess maybe I have. I didn't know getting married was such a big job. There has been my trousseau to prepare, linens to embroider, dresses to have made. Plus all the work of the household. I am tired. And I've probably been sharp with you."

"You have been," Annie said with a shrug. "But maybe if I was seventeen, I'd be sharp with me too." She laughed, then added, "Doesn't it seem like we're always getting ready for Father to come home? I hope he'll stay this time." She thought for a bit and said, "We just won't be sad while Father's here. Then maybe he won't be eager to leave again."

Patsy shook her head. "Annie, Father doesn't leave because he's eager to get away. Father loves Scotchtown, but business calls him. He can't say no." She thought for a moment. "You are right. We can try to make his stay here pleasant. You must try to be more of a lady. Don't give us reasons to worry about you and fret over you."

Young Annie felt guilty as she thought about the wet dress lying in the hamper and Mrs. Thacker's muddy cloak hanging in the wardrobe. She stared at the floor.

Patsy puttered with their mother's tea chest as she spoke. "My only comfort is that Father will surely see that you need to act more like a lady and less like one of Uncle William's Indians," she said, referring to her uncle who lived in the western wilderness. "He's bound to buy you new dresses soon—and they'll have hoops or bustles. Surely that will slow you down."

"But I don't want to wear hoops yet," Annie said. "You can't ride a horse in hoops; you can't hike; you can't run; you can't play. That's no fun, Patsy."

Her older sister sighed. "I gave up fun years ago— ever since Mama's been ill. It's about time you helped with some of the burden," she said. "You are too much like Father for your own good. It may be okay for a man to have strong opinions and go on about them. But you have to be practical. You've got to learn to sew and tend to matters in a big house. That's the kind of job the good Lord is going to give you. And Father better tell you so— though he probably won't." Patsy looked resigned. "Now get a move on. You go upstairs and play with Elizabeth and Edward."

Only too glad to get away from Patsy, Annie ran up the stairs to the big room—the site of the harvest party. There she found Elizabeth and Edward asleep with their nurse sitting close by.

Annie settled herself in front of a window from which she could see the road that would bring her father home again. She daydreamed, not about fancy dresses, but about the fish that got away.

4

FATHER'S SECRET MEETING

LAUGHTER ROSE FROM THE DINING ROOM TO THE nursery above where Annie had been served dinner with Edward and Elizabeth. Her father had returned yesterday. Today he was entertaining friends and political figures from Hanover County. Although she sat at the top of the stairs straining to hear the conversation below, she heard little more than an occasional burst of laughter. "Not fair," she said with exasperation. "William, Patsy, and John shouldn't be able to stay with Father while I'm sent off to be with the babies." But Annie knew her father would tolerate no complaints. "Your time will come," he was fond of saying to her.

Annie crept down the stairs and into the family dining room. It was next door to the formal dining room where the guests had been served dinner. But now that dinner was over, her father had taken his guests into the gentlemen's parlor. Patsy had already gone into her room for the night.

The large table was still set, she found as she entered the formal dining room. Glasses glowed in the firelight, a half-eaten pecan pie sat on the table.

Annie cut a piece and put it on a clean plate. She absentmindedly picked at the pie, savoring the sweet brown custard and the crunchy nut topping. When she finished that piece, she debated having another. Having decided no, Annie was in a dilemma. She could go to bed as Patsy had done, but she wanted news from Philadelphia, and she knew she wouldn't hear it if she was sleeping. She peeked out into the central hall. Its dark wood floors, worn by the constant traffic, gleamed softly in the lantern light. Annie walked carefully toward the gentlemen's parlor, giggling nervously. "I feel like I'm a spy for the king of England," she thought.

The parlor door was shut tight. Only muffled voices floated through the thick, walnut panels. Annie crouched outside the door, her head pressed against it. She could hear John Fontaine's voice and Father's muffled response. But nothing more than that.

Just then, the back door opened. A servant carrying a large stack of books and papers from her father's law office tried to make his way through the heavy door. Annie darted back across the hall into the dining room before the servant could turn around. She watched as he carried the papers to the parlor and knocked. The door opened. Warm light spilled out of the room into the dim hallway. The smell of tobacco drifted out of the room, and a tumble of deep voices broke the silence.

Waiting until the servant left before slipping back into the hall, Annie retraced her steps to the parlor only to find that the servant had not shut the door all the way. It remained cracked about six inches. She settled herself next to the door and sat Indian-fashion with her head leaning on crossed arms and listened.

"Richard and John, I appreciate the work you've done in managing affairs here while I've been away," Henry said. "Have the boys been studying?"

"They aren't as diligent in their studies as they might be," the tutor, Richard Dabney, replied.

"Nor was I," laughed the elder Henry. "My parents despaired that I'd ever make a success in life. But the law has been good to me. It rewards my gift of gab," he said. "Well, the harvest looks good, the children healthy . . . . I'm satisfied."

"Will you tell us about events in Philadelphia?"

Annie tensed. She didn't recognize the speaker's voice, so she put her head a little closer to the door.

"It was a good convention. The Virginia delegation was divided at first. Richard Henry Lee and I more firm in our aim to stand up to England, others believing that we could still avoid war and compromise with the English governor and the king. But meeting with our brothers from Massachusetts, Pennsylvania, New York, and elsewhere sparked a change of thinking. We are no longer separate colonies dealing with the Crown. We are united as colonies. Our interests are the same."

"What was decided?"

"Sam Adams introduced resolutions that were accepted. All of us, not just the good folks of Massachusetts, are going to resist the Intolerable Acts."

Annie knew that the Intolerable Acts had been forced on the people of Boston as payment for the Boston Tea Party, where men disguised as Indians had thrown all the British tea into the harbor rather than pay a tax on it.

Patrick Henry continued, "The colonies agreed not to pay taxes to the Crown. And we agreed not to import any British goods. Finally, we agreed that Britain has no authority over us except in regulating trade. It was a courageous convention; these are bold steps."

"What do you think? Will Britain drive us to the brink? And if there is war, what will be the result?" John Fontaine asked.

Goosebumps chased up Annie's spine. War. Such an awesome word. She listened carefully for her father's reply.

"My frank opinion is that we will have war. England will drive us to the edge. No compromise will take place, fighting will soon begin, and the war will be bloody."

Again, John Fontaine spoke. "But do you think that an

infant nation such as ours, without guns, ships, or money to get them—do you still think it is possible that we could win against the superior power of Great Britain?"

Paying close attention, Annie heard her father say, "I will be honest with you. I doubt that alone we will be able to win. But what about France? or Spain? or Holland? They are the natural enemies of Great Britain. Do you think they will stand idle? No! They will fight for us. And I am convinced that we shall be victorious and our independence shall be established, and we shall take our stand among the nations of the earth."

"Hotheads like Sam Adams have brought us to this point." Again the strange voice.

"Sam Adams is a good man. He sees things clearly, and he works from principle. Some things, my friend, are worth fighting for." Patrick Henry sounded like a preacher as he spoke. His voice was soft, but it was hard with conviction.

The strange voice sounded harsher. "This cause is not one of those things. The Bible is clear that we are to submit to the proper authorities. I've not seen the Crown removed from authority."

"Francis, I'm sorry that you and I are in disagreement here. I should not have spoken so bluntly, nor would I have, if I had known your sentiments. It may be that God is raising up new authorities—the House of Burgessess, the Continental Congress. We aren't criminals. We are law-abiding men seeking to protect and save our liberties in the face of a tyrant."

Annie hadn't heard her father speak like this before. A chair scraped, and she heard the heavy sound of boots crossing the floor. Then Patrick Henry spoke again, "We might still remain friends, Francis. Perhaps we will be in agreement someday."

The response came sharp with anger. "It's not possible to be friends with a traitor. My honor won't permit it. I pray that you pull back, Patrick, while there is yet time. And your duty surely lies elsewhere than on this foolish course you are taking. Give my regards to Patsy and your wife. Good day."

Annie scooted back into the shadows away from the door. From her position she watched as Francis Doyle, a distant cousin and a lawyer, stalked out the front door. The parlor door remained open as he had left it. She crept in front of the door and caught a glimpse of her father, his back turned toward the huge corner fireplace, absent-mindedly stirring the wood with a poker.

John Fontaine interrupted the silence. "I'm surprised at Francis. And I'm worried. Do you think he'll make trouble for you?"

"I don't know. He's always been hotheaded—and certain that he's right. A good man if he's on your side. But no friend if he's not. I'm not sure that our years of friendship and our family connection will mean anything to him if he's convinced I've sold out to the devil, which is what he considers Sam Adams to be."

"Do we need to watch him?"

"What can he do? If he informs Lord Governor Dunmore that I'm plotting treason—well, it won't be news to Dunmore. When I start raising a militia, which I plan to do this month, the news will get to the governor soon enough. Courage! We'll all need it in the days ahead. I don't think we need to worry more about Francis Doyle. Now, I've had a hard week. I'm tired. I think I will retire."

Annie had crept back to her place near the wall. She felt drowsy and decided to stretch out, her arms pillowing her head. "I'll just close my eyes for a minute," she thought. The next thing she knew she was awakened by the sound of footsteps.

"I thought my little Annie would be there," Patrick Henry said with a laugh. "You think you'll miss some excitement if you go to bed?"

Annie blushed while her father reached down and tousled her hair. He lowered his lanky body next to hers. "It's bedtime. The guests have left. Come, child. We'll have time to talk tomorrow."

Annie rubbed her eyes with one hand and held her father's hand tight in her other.

Her father continued speaking: "It's been hard for you, hasn't it? With me away and Patsy in charge . . . . I'm sorry, but sometimes things don't work out as we might hope . . . ." A look of such sadness came over Patrick Henry's face that Annie couldn't speak. She rested her head against his chest while he put his arm around her.

"I went downstairs to visit your mama a while ago. She looked better, I think. Would you like to go with me to see her tomorrow?"

"Oh, Father. I'd like to see her. Patsy said I couldn't while you were away . . . ." Tears began to stream down Annie's cheek. "She said I'd make Mama worse, but I wouldn't have, would I?"

"No, my sweet, I don't think you would make your mama worse. She's in God's hands now. I'm afraid that only He can make her better—or worse. You mustn't be too hard on Patsy, though. She's had a heavy load. She should be thinking about parties and dresses; instead she's been saddled with this house and responsibility. God knows it's a big job, and she's done her best. Without Patsy I don't think I could have gone to Philadelphia. Men count on me . . . and I count on Patsy. You'll have to help her."

A flash of jealousy surged in Annie. Father was talking as though Patsy was doing important work for Virginia . . . what was Annie doing? She straightened up. "I can be a big help too, Father. You'll see. I will be every bit as much help as Patsy."

Patrick Henry laughed and pulled his daughter up. "I know you will be a help. But first you need your sleep."

5

ANNIE'S FALL

THE NEXT MORNING PATRICK HENRY GREETED YOUNG Annie on the back steps. "Hurry, girl. We've got a lot to do today. Get something warm on. We're going to look over the farm."

Annie ran to her room and put on a soft woolen cape that fit snugly around her neck. She wore leather gloves and put on her warm winter boots. She ran out to the stables where her father was already talking to the groom.

"Here she is," he announced as Annie ran up. "Saddle up old Paint for her, Joseph."

Joseph led Paint, a small brown horse, out of his stall. He threw a blanket on the animal's back, then lifted the heavy, well-oiled saddle. Annie stood near Paint's head, patting the smooth neck with her arms, ducking her head when the horse tried to nibble on her hair.

"Okay, up you go," her father said, and he lifted

Annie into the saddle. She settled herself in the sidesaddle, her heavy skirts falling on one side of the horse. Patrick Henry mounted his own horse, a big black gelding, and they rode past the kitchen toward the slave quarters and the blacksmith shop.

"Look at that hay, Annie," her father said. "Looks like a good harvest. Scotchtown has done us proud this year." Henry surveyed his farm with pride.

Annie also gazed over the farm. Her glance settled on the cottages where the slaves lived. Even though the buildings were clean and well-maintained, Annie didn't like them. "Why must we have slaves?" she asked her father in a quiet voice. "I wouldn't like to be sold like a sack of flour."

Patrick Henry didn't answer at first. He spurred his horse and galloped ahead, then reined the horse around until he was walking with Annie once again. Only the clip-clopping of the horses' hooves broke the silence. Finally, he spoke.

"I cannot justify having slaves," he said slowly. "Slavery is an awful thing. It is against the Bible and destructive of liberty. Every honest thinking man rejects it . . . ."

"Then why do we keep slaves?" Annie demanded. "Shouldn't we free them? Isn't that our duty?"

Patrick Henry shook his head sadly. "I find it hard to believe I am the master of slaves of my own purchase. But,

I must confess, I am drawn along by the inconvenience of living here without them."

As he spoke, the two came in sight of the stable. "I'm sorry I can't ride longer now, Annie, but I must do some work. We'll visit your mother later." He dismounted and strode to his office without waiting for a response.

Annie stared at her father's back. She was angry. Joseph reached up to help her down, but Annie shook her head. "I'm going to ride a little longer," she said.

Giving the horse a good kick, she turned him back towards the pasture. The horse was eager to run. Annie clutched tightly to the reins and the horse's mane. The wind bit her face. Branches reached out and scratched her, but she ignored them. Her father's words echoed in her head like the clopping of the horse's hooves. Slavery was wrong, Father knew it, and yet he kept them anyway.

Up ahead a tree had fallen over the path. Annie looked at it with determination. "Jump it, Paint," she urged the horse, kicking him sharply with her boot. Paint picked up speed and cleared the trunk, but Annie flew off and landed in a ditch at the side of the path. She lay there, stunned. When she tried to move, a sharp pain ran up her arm. "Oh, Lord," she cried. "Help me."

Paint stood over her, neighing softly. Annie wiggled her toes. Nothing was wrong with them. Then she shifted her legs. They were sore, but there was no sharp pain.

With her good arm, Annie forced herself into a sitting position. She surveyed the situation. She was far from home, alone, with an injured arm. And it would be cold tonight. She had to get back to Scotchtown, but how would she get there?

The first thing she must do was tie her arm against her body so that it couldn't move. Annie looked at her skirt. It was already torn from the fall. She grabbed the hem with her good hand and tugged until the skirt began to tear. Soon she had a strip about four feet long. Tucking the end under her injured arm, she wrapped the strip around her back, under her good arm, and over the bad one as many times as she could. Then she tied the end. Now the injured arm was held snugly against her.

Next she whistled for Paint who had wandered off to graze. Annie reached up and grabbed the horse's reins, which were trailing in the dirt. She used them to pull herself up until she was standing, a little shakily, next to the horse.

"Now, Paint," she whispered. "You've got to get me home." Annie knew she couldn't pull herself into the sidesaddle without help. Even when she was healthy, her father or Joseph helped her. By herself, with an injured arm, it would be impossible. But a nearby stump offered hope. She led the horse to it and climbed up. From the stump, the injured girl put one foot in the stirrup. But could she lift herself? She grabbed the saddle horn with her good hand and pulled. Again she prayed, "God help me. Give me strength."

It took several tries, but finally Annie was in the saddle. She leaned over and spoke softly to the horse. "Take me home, Paint."

The horse responded as though he knew something was wrong. He picked his way carefully around the ruts and rocks so that Annie wouldn't be bumped and jarred. Before too long they were back within sight of the house.

Patrick Henry must have seen her approach because he was waiting for Annie at the stables. When he saw that she was hurt, he rushed to her, calling behind to Joseph, "Get the horse and ring the bell." Reaching up, her father gently lifted Annie from the saddle, careful not to touch her injured arm.

"Tell me what happened," he said softly.

Annie couldn't speak at first. But when she saw her father's frightened expression, she took a deep breath and smiled. He carried her into the house and laid her gently on her bed. Patsy hovered anxiously nearby asking what had happened. He shushed her, then sat down by Annie's side.

"You have to tell us what happened, Annie."

Annie sighed. "We were galloping. I asked Paint to

jump. He did, but I fell off. I think I've broken my arm," Annie said.

"Patsy, we must have the doctor. Send John over to Doctor Payne's. He must not delay," their father ordered.

Patsy ran from the room. Her face was drawn with worry.

Reaching for her father's hand with her good hand, she said, "I'm sorry, Father. I didn't mean to be trouble. I was angry with you, and I foolishly ran."

"Annie, you aren't trouble. I'm sorry that I have feet of clay. But no one knows it better than I. If it makes you feel better, I think a time will come when we can be rid of slavery. And until that time comes, we must treat those in our care with kindness and gentleness. You will not see one of our slaves mistreated on this farm. That is a promise."

Annie smiled weakly. Her arm ached, and she felt unnaturally tired. "Why won't you let me sleep, Father," she said when he continued to talk to her.

"You must not sleep until the doctor comes, little one. I'll amuse you with stories from Philadelphia. But you may not sleep."

Patrick Henry talked on as Annie drifted in and out of sleep. Finally, the doctor arrived. He examined the arm and announced, "A clean break. I'll set it in a splint. It will heal good as new, or nearly so, if you are careful."

Annie smiled and lay back on her pillow. She heard

Patsy's gentle voice urging her to drink a sour-tasting potion the doctor said would prevent fever. She drank it and drifted off to sleep while her father sat anxiously at her side.

6

"REJOICE THE SOUL OF THY SERVANT"

EVEN THOUGH SHE FELT BETTER, ANNIE WASN'T allowed out of bed for a week. Her father said firmly, "You won't miss anything if you stay in bed, and it's one way I can guarantee that you won't get into trouble."

Annie read a little and sketched until she didn't want to see another pencil. Occasionally her father brought his violin into the room and played. Sometimes the boys brought in cards—but Annie didn't know the games they played. Even Elizabeth tried to entertain her. She brought her dollies and their dishes into Annie's room and together they played house. Elizabeth smiled a lot. "I like it when you are sick, Annie. Then you play with me," she said.

But finally, on December 1, Patrick Henry announced that his daughter Annie was to get up and dressed. More than that, he had a surprise. "You're going to see your mama today, Annie. You asked me last week, before the accident, and I've been waiting until you were strong enough. But I think you must see her now."

Annie dressed awkwardly. Patsy had altered several dresses by opening up the left sleeve to make room for the splint, but it was hard for Annie to pull the dress on. Finally, though, she was dressed and ready to go.

The stairs where he waited for her were outside at the end of the house near the kitchen. The stairs led into the basement which was divided, on this half of the house, into four rooms. Patrick Henry and his daughter walked down the few steps into the basement. The brick floor was cold beneath their feet. Windows near the ceiling let in plenty of light, but the low ceilings forced him to stoop slightly. He peeked into one room where a woman sat knitting .

"Tildy, I want to take Annie in to see Mrs. Henry. How is she today?"

Tildy's eyes swept from her master's face to Annie's. "She's not good, Master Henry. She's not good. But she's as good as she ever is. There's no reason not to let the child see her. Might do her some good, though I don't know about that."

Clutching her father's hand even tighter, Annie could feel the course calluses on his palm. At that moment a high pitched moan erupted from the room. Patrick Henry smiled encouragingly. "It will be fine. Come along, Annie." He led her gently into the room and whispered in her ear, "Don't be afraid. It is your mama, even if she doesn't look like it."

Annie took a deep breath and walked toward the rocking chair, turned so its back faced the door. Her father led her by the hand around to the front of the rocker. Sarah Henry was bound by a straight dress. It's heavy cotton strips held her arms at her side, so she was unable to get up from her chair. Her head fell limply to the side, her mouth hung slack, and a bit of spittle dripped from the corner. Frightening moans came from her mother's lips, but Sarah Henry seemed unaware of them. Annie recoiled from the woman in front of her. She found it hard to believe that this creature was the same mother whose eyes were once warm and alive and whose touch had comforted Annie when she was hurt.

She tried to back away from the chair, but her father's firm grip held her in place. He pushed her toward her mother's chair whispering, "Say something."

Annie obeyed hesitantly. "Hello, Mama," she said softly. "I've missed you so much."

Her mother didn't respond or give any sign that she had heard the girl speak. Annie didn't know what else to do. She looked to her father for guidance.

"Sarah, dear, I thought it would do you good to see Annie. I know it pains you to be far from your children,"

Patrick said. "I thought we could visit for a while before going back upstairs."

He tried to talk about the farm and the family. He mentioned his trip to Philadelphia and Patsy's upcoming wedding, but Sarah Henry's expression never changed.

"Let me read you a Psalm, Sarah," he said gently as he pulled a little pocket psalter from his vest. "Bow down thine ear, O Lord, hear me: for I am poor and needy. Preserve my soul; for I am holy: O thou my God, save thy servant that trusteth in thee. Be merciful unto me, O Lord: for I cry unto thee daily. Rejoice the soul of thy servant: for unto thee, O Lord, do I lift up my soul."

When Annie heard the words "Rejoice the soul of thy servant" she could stand it no longer. A huge sob rose up from her chest and racked her shoulders. She began to weep until her throat hurt and her eyes were swollen.

Minutes went by. She wiped her tears and looked up at her mother. Tears fell from the silent woman's eyes unchecked. Then Annie looked at her father. He held Sarah's hand, and he too was crying.

A bit later, Annie sat at the dining room table across from her father. Light from the candles played across his face, highlighting the wrinkles. He looked older, she thought. Tired.

"Daddy, what's wrong with Mama? Is she going to get better?" Annie asked.

Patrick looked up at his daughter and shook his head sadly. "Your mama's very sick. She's got a head sickness. She doesn't know who she is; she doesn't know who we are . . . . I don't know if she'll get better."

"But maybe if she came upstairs . . . maybe it is being shut up downstairs that's making her sick," Annie whispered, afraid to criticize her father's decision to keep Sarah Henry in the basement.

The shadow of a smile flitted across Patrick Henry's face. "Honey, the reason your mama stays downstairs with Tildy is so she won't hurt herself or someone else. We don't want to send your mama to the asylum. Here we know she'll be loved and cared for. She is my wife, after all. She is your mama. It's the least we can do."

"But why, Daddy, why is Mama sick?"

"Honey, I don't know why God does what he does. Sometimes His ways are mysterious. But won't the Judge of all the world do what is right?"

Annie was quiet. She didn't know the answer to the question. "I can't believe that it is right that Mama is sick."

Patrick Henry asked, "Annie, do you remember the fire?

His daughter nodded.

"A great deal of wheat was destroyed. We asked why God would do that? But I've learned two things from that fire. First, God sometimes has to teach us how much we must depend on Him. Sometimes we think we are in control of our lives, of this marvelous farm, of events. But God wants us to understand that it comes from Him. And second, sometimes these bad things, like the fire, can actually produce something good. John Fontaine tells me that all of the ash in the soil will make that field even more fertile next year. God made a good thing come out of that fire."

Patrick Henry patted her hand. "Come, let's find Patsy."

The next morning, Annie didn't want to get up. She didn't want to see her father and she didn't want to see Patsy. Rumbling in her stomach, however, reminded her that she was hungry. She reluctantly washed and dressed herself.

When she came into the dining room, everyone else had already eaten. Patsy hovered over Annie. "Are you sure you are well? Should I send for the doctor?" she asked.

"I didn't want to get up," Annie grumbled. "That's all."

"Then you won't eat," Patsy said.

Annie scowled. Then she realized that she had no cause to be angry with Patsy. This trouble was part of God's plan for Patrick Henry's house. "I'm sorry, Patsy. I am hungry. Is it too late for breakfast?"

Patsy set a plate of food before Annie. Then she asked, "Was it awful seeing Mama?"

Annie nodded. "I didn't know it would be so bad. I thought Mama was getting better. I can't bear to think of her down there, all alone except for Tildy."

"Mama's not alone," Patsy said. "When Father is home he goes down everyday. And Mrs. Thacker comes often. She'll be here this morning, I think. Besides, Mama doesn't know who visits and who doesn't."

After finishing her breakfast in silence, Annie went into her bedroom and found Mrs. Thacker's cloak, now cleaned and brushed. She took it with her to a spot under the lilac bush outside Mama's window. Annie sat at the base of it, ignoring the way the dry branches poked at her back. After a while, she saw their new neighbor come around the side of the house and enter the door to the basement as though she had done it many times.

About a half hour later she came out, waved at Tildy, and called out that she'd come again on Friday. Annie waited until Mrs. Thacker was halfway across the front yard then ran after her. She was breathless when she reached the woman's side.

Mrs. Thacker looked down. "Annie, I didn't see you," she said, and continued walking. "Whatever happened to your arm?"

"I fell off a horse," Annie said. "But I'm fine now."

She held out the cloak. "I wanted to return this to you. Thank you."

"You're welcome," Mrs. Thacker replied as she took the cloak.

Annie tried to keep up, but Mrs. Thacker's stride was too long, so Annie trotted and skipped beside her. "How was Mama today?" she asked, biting her lower lip nervously.

"Oh, I didn't see much difference. She was quiet. She listened when I read a Psalm. She didn't scream out." Mrs. Thacker spoke matter-of-factly as though Annie was an adult and able to understand.

"Does Mama know you?" Annie asked.

Mrs. Thacker smiled. "I don't think she knows me now. But we used to know each other. We grew up near each other, not far from here. I've known Sarah Shelton for a long time."

"But if she doesn't know you, why do you come?" Annie persisted.

"I guess I come because I love your mama, and I want her to cling to the truth. I believe your mama understands some of what we tell her, at least I pray she does."

They walked together quietly. Mrs. Thacker slowed her pace so that Annie no longer had to trot to keep up.

Finally Annie asked the question that had bothered her all night, "Father says God can turn this sickness into good. Do you believe that?"

Mrs. Thacker paused. She looked at Annie's serious face and understood the struggle the young girl was having. "Let's sit for a minute," she said, lowering herself to the ground. "That's a hard question, isn't it? How can God, if He's good, let such bad things happen?" Mrs. Thacker paused, then asked, "Do you know the story of Joseph?"

Annie blushed. She knew she should know the story and had certainly heard it. She shook her head shyly.

"You don't know the Joseph story? That's one of the most exciting stories in the whole Bible. I can't imagine what your daddy . . . . Oh, never mind. Well, it goes like this:

"Joseph was a young man—oh, about Patsy's age, I'd say. He was his daddy's favorite because he had been born when his daddy was getting on in years. One time, Joseph's daddy gave Joseph a special coat of many colors. That made Joseph's brothers—he had eleven of them—angry. They believed their daddy loved Joseph best."

"Like Father loves Patsy," Annie interrupted.

"Shhh . . . . Just listen to the story," Mrs. Thacker replied.

"One day he had a dream. It was about Joseph and his brothers binding up sheaves of grain in the field. Suddenly, in the dream, the brothers' sheaves of grain gathered around Joseph's grain and bowed down to it. As you can imagine, the brothers didn't like that dream. And then Joseph had another dream where the sun, the moon and the stars all bowed down to him. Of course, he told his brothers this dream also. They got even angrier. They didn't even like to talk to him."

"But what's this got to do with bad things being good?" asked Annie.

"Be patient, child. You'll see," Mrs. Thacker answered.

"One day Jacob told Joseph to go out to his brothers who were watching the flocks of sheep. Joseph went. His brothers saw him from a distance, and do you know what they decided to do? They decided to kill him.

"But Reuben, the oldest, had second thoughts. He convinced the brothers not to kill Joseph but to throw him into a pit instead. So that's what they did. But first they took Joseph's beautiful coat.

"You'd think Joseph's brothers would be feeling pretty bad. Maybe they'd change their minds. But these brothers sat down and ate a meal. And while they were eating, some traders came by. The brothers had another idea. They sold Joseph to the traders.

"Then they killed an animal, dipped Joseph's coat into the blood, and took the bloody coat back to Jacob. 'He's dead,' they told Jacob. 'A lion got him.'"

"That's awful," Annie said. "I'd never do that to Patsy."

"No, I don't think you would," Mrs. Thacker laughed. "That was very wicked."

"What happened next?" Annie asked.

"Well, those traders sold Joseph into slavery in Egypt where he eventually became a trusted servant. But the wife of his master accused Joseph of wickedness. It wasn't true, of course, but Joseph was thrown in jail where he stayed a long time.

"A while later Pharaoh, the king of Egypt, had some dreams. He asked everyone to help him figure out what the dreams meant. No one could do it. But one of the men from prison remembered that Joseph knew about dreams. He told Pharaoh about him."

Annie leaned forward to hear the story. Mrs. Thacker's voice gained strength as she told it.

"Joseph was able to tell Pharaoh his dream. He told him there would be seven years of plenty followed by seven years of famine.

"The king asked Joseph what he should do, and Joseph told him to store the grain during the good years so they'd have enough to eat during the bad ones."

"But how is this good?" Annie asked.

"I'm almost there, child. Be patient. Be patient. Well, the Pharaoh did what Joseph said. In fact, he put Joseph in charge. Everything Joseph said came true. When the bad years came, people from all around had to come to Joseph to ask for food because he had stored the grain. And do you know who came? Joseph's brothers. Only they didn't know it was Joseph. They thought he was dead. After a while, Joseph revealed himself to his brothers."

"I bet he was angry with them. He probably wouldn't sell them any grain," Annie said.

"Oh no . . . . He gave them grain. In fact, he didn't take their money. And when he told them who he was, he cried. But you know what Joseph said to them when they said they were sorry. He said—and here's my point, Annie—'ye thought evil against me; but God meant it unto good.' That means that they meant it for evil, but God meant it for good. You see, if Joseph's brothers hadn't sold him into slavery, Joseph wouldn't have been in Egypt to read the king's dream. The Pharaoh wouldn't have prepared for the famine, and all the people, including Joseph and his brothers, would have starved. That's how God can take bad—even evil things—and bring good out of them."

"But what about Mama?" Annie asked. "How can that be good?"

Mrs. Thacker shook her head sadly. "I don't know. I truly don't know. There is a promise that God works things out for the good of those who love Him. But it isn't always clear to us when we are in the midst of trouble. Your mother loves the Lord. You must make sure you do also."

She stood up and brushed the dry grass off her skirt. "I've got to hurry home, Annie. We'll talk again."

Annie turned back toward Scotchtown. She felt at loose ends wondering where her father had gone. She read for a while, but found she couldn't concentrate. Then she went for a walk, but the sights and smells that usually amused her had no interest. Finally, she found herself outside the kitchen door. A good smell of fried cakes came from inside. Annie followed the smell.

Her brother John was sitting at the heavy plank table with a cup of cider and a plate of cakes in front of him. He looked up when his younger sister with the broken arm entered the room. "Have some fried cakes. They're plenty good," he said, waving a donut in the air.

Annie sat next to him and took the offered donut. A fire blazed in the fireplace. Cast iron pots hung near the flames with soup cooking for dinner. A chicken roasted on a spit. The good smells of food filled the air.

"Do you know where Father went?" Annie asked her brother.

"Yep."

"Well, aren't you going to tell me?" she asked impatiently.

"I guess if Father wanted you to know, he'd have told you himself," John said.

"You are so infuriating. Of course he couldn't tell me. He couldn't find me," Annie said, trying to keep her patience.

"Were you lost?" John asked with a mock tone of concern.

Annie slapped the table hard with her good hand.

Her brother laughed. "You better watch out or you will hurt your good hand. I'll tell you where he's gone. I was only teasing. He's gone to raise an army—or a militia. He took William with him." John sounded angry about that. "Said I wasn't old enough yet."

Annie laughed. "Where'd they meet?"

"Smith's Tavern, of course. They're going to meet there often and practice. I can't believe I can't go. I have to stay around here with women." John shuddered when he thought of the humiliation.

Annie laughed again. "I'm not going to wait."

"Where are you going?" John asked.

"I'm going to Smith's Tavern," Annie answered smugly. "You may be too young to march, but you aren't too young to watch—and neither am I. How will we ever know what's going on if we stay around here? Let's ask Joseph to hook up the wagon. You can drive."

John's mouth opened to protest. Then he grinned. "Let's go. Beat you to the stable."

7

CHRISTMAS

INTER WAS A GOOD TIME TO RAISE A MILITIA. THERE was less work for farmers to do once they had harvested their crops and sent their wheat to John Syme's mill where it was ground into flour and packed for sale. Tobacco had been gathered, dried and prepared for shipping, and the hogs were butchered.

Patrick Henry and his neighbors traveled to Smith's Tavern often. They called it muster day when all the men paraded. They came in their plowing clothes, their muddy boots tapping out the count on the hard-packed field. Children also marched with sticks instead of muskets while ladies gathered in groups to gossip.

After that first day, Annie rode into Hanover, the nearest village, whenever her father said she could. Her splint had been removed, and although the arm was stiff, she was able to use it a little. The doctor said it would improve with time.

At the square, Annie flitted from group to group. Some days she marched with the boys, tucking her hair into a cap and ignoring their groans of protest. Other times she played hoops and balls with the younger children, and sometimes she stood with the ladies, listening to them talk about the price of sugar, or who still had tea or good English fabric. None of those products was allowed into the colonies anymore.

Amidst the marching, Christmas, 1774, came to Scotchtown. Its arrival took everyone by surprise. The house had taken on an air of neglect since fall. Patsy Henry was busy with the day-to-day running of the household and plans for her springtime wedding, and Patrick Henry's attention was focused on the militia. Annie figured it must be almost Christmas. The first snow had fallen and melted, leaving nothing behind but clumps of dirty ice.

Still, she didn't think it fitting to have a celebration with her mother so sick. Sometimes she stood outside the window to her mother's room and listened, hoping that her mother might get well and the family might return to normal. But that didn't happen. On good days there was no sound from the window. More often, there was more awful moaning and screaming. Then she'd hear Tildy's soft voice soothing and comforting away her mother's tears.

One day, their father strode into the family dining room where the children were having supper. He said, "The work is done. It's time to gather some greens and dress up the house for Christmas."

Annie glanced at Patsy. She figured Patsy would say what Annie was thinking: "It's not right to think about Christmas and celebrating, what with Mama being so sick and all." But Patsy didn't say it. Instead she smiled at their father as though he were a child to be humored and said, "It's too cold for me. We don't have to decorate this year."

"Nonsense. Christmas comes but once a year, and we are going to mark the day. On Christmas we'll be feasting, and we'll not do it in a house that looks more like it's in mourning than in celebration. Your mother won't be offended." He turned to Annie. "How about you? Won't you come with me?"

Annie didn't want to go—but time alone with her father was rare. She grudgingly nodded but made no move to join him.

"Well, goosey. If you want to go, get a move on. It's going to snow. You can feel it. I want to be back before it does. I'll have Joseph harness the wagon. You dress warmly."

Annie put on her warmest coat and heavy wool stockings under her thick leather boots. She tied a scarf over her head and tucked her hands into Patsy's fur muffler.

She waited on the porch for Joseph to bring the wagon around. An icy wind chilled her even through her heavy coat.

Her father came out of the house in his stained, old buckskin coat and a fur cap. His woolen breeches showed signs of wear.

Annie laughed with delight when she saw him. "You look like Uncle William," she said.

He smiled as he lifted Annie into the wagon and wrapped a heavy fur blanket around her legs. Annie's feet rested on heated bricks. "You know, I didn't always wear fancy clothes," he said. "Folks used to wonder whether I'd show up in court in buckskins."

Annie remembered those days vaguely—before they had bought Scotchtown, before Patrick Henry had become wealthy from his work as a lawyer, before Mama had taken sick. Somehow the sight of the old clothes made Annie sad and wishing for the old days.

A knot settled in her stomach. Her father reached over and squeezed Annie's thin shoulders, but he said nothing. The horse made its way quickly over the frozen ground until they entered the pine forest.

"Let's see. What do we need? Greens for the windows, surely. That's eight wreaths across the front. We'll need a wagon load of branches to make that many wreaths."

Patrick Henry hopped out. He used a small hatchet to remove limbs from the pines. Annie sat in the wagon feeling the bite of the wind through her coat. She wished she had stayed with Patsy. Her father loaded the limbs into the back of the wagon. He glanced at Annie huddled on the bench. "I think I'll just chop a whole tree down," he said. "We can remove the limbs at home.

He climbed up on the wagon and clucked to the horses. "I want to find one big enough to do the job. Let's go a bit further."

They rode on until they came to a stand of 12-foot trees. Annie felt a quickening of excitement in spite of herself. "Oh, one of these please, Father," she pleaded. "They are beautiful."

He smiled. "That's what I thought," he agreed. Taking his ax, he climbed down.

"Stand back," he called to his daughter. "These chips will fly into your eyes."

He raised the heavy ax over his shoulders and swung it with terrific force. The tree shuddered. Over and over again he hit the trunk with the ax, harder and harder. Annie shrunk back as she watched her father swing so hard. He was strong, she knew that. But he was also angry, and he was pouring out his anger on that tree. The tree finally fell over with a thud. He wiped the sweat from his forehead with his sleeve. Annie couldn't speak. She watched her father load it onto the back of the wagon. He then lifted Annie back into her seat. "We'd best be getting home now. Snow's coming," he added, looking up at the heavy gray canopy of clouds.

As they rode back to Scotchtown, her father said, "This reminds me of the first winter Sarah and I were married. We had no money and a baby on the way. We were living with Grandma Shelton who thought we'd done a fool thing to marry so young. No matter. That Christmas, your mama and I took the wagon out and cut down a tree. We dragged it back to Grandma Shelton's, pleased that we were going to have enough greens to decorate the whole house.

"But, Grandma Shelton wasn't too happy about it. Said she didn't much cotton to all this pagan decorating. She was of the old school—no point in setting up Christmas as any more important than any other day. Just leads to bad habits, she warned us. Well, Sarah and I sat in that wagon with that old pine tree and just laughed. We got a candle and lit it, sang a few carols, drank some cider, and had our own celebration."

Annie had never heard her father talk about the old days. She felt tears burning the back of her eyelids. She squeezed her eyes shut to keep the tears from running down her cheek.

He kissed her gently on her forehead. "Your mama used to be a beautiful woman. That's how I want to remember her." He sighed.

That evening Patrick Henry took out his fiddle. He gathered the children into his parlor and said, "We are going to sing. Annie, find the hymnal." While she found the book, her father played his violin. He said to Patsy, "Come, show this family how to dance." He played and she danced until everyone was clapping hands and stomping feet. Little Elizabeth ran to her father's knee. "Daddy, Daddy, dance with me," she said. He stood up, his lanky form towering over his little daughter. "I'd be delighted. Patsy, will you play the harpsichord?"

As Patsy played, Patrick Henry danced with his daughters, first Elizabeth, then Annie. Finally, he fell back into a chair. "Enough. That's enough. I'm an old man and can't dance anymore." He hushed the protests with his hand. Then he looked at the glowing faces surrounding him. "This family has been without laughter too long. We won't go so long again," he said. "I promise. Now let's sing some hymns."

Annie glanced at the family gathered in the parlor. Father sat in his armchair near the fire, baby Edward on one knee, Elizabeth on the other. John Fontaine stood near Patsy at the harpsichord. William and John sat on the floor, their long legs stretched out before them. Mr. Dabney, the tutor, was on the settee. Annie figured she would never forget that night—familiar faces made visible by the lamplight, the sweet smell of apple logs burning in the fireplace, and Father's rich baritone voice singing the words, "Joy to the World, the Lord is Come."

Later in her room, snuggled down into the warm comforter, she prayed. "Lord, please make Mama better." Hot tears stung her eyes. She didn't fight them. That night she cried for Mama, Daddy, and for herself.

8

ANDREW THACKER

FEBRUARY WAS MARKED BY AN UNBROKEN STRING of bleak, gray days. The temperature stayed just above freezing, turning whatever snow there was to gray and brown slush.

One cold, drizzly day toward the end of February, Annie had taken refuge upstairs with Elizabeth and Edward. A children's tea party was in progress. She set the table, brought up those biscuits called scones, and poured tea—actually warm apple cider.

Her younger sister and brother happily sipped the cider and fed small cakes to the gathered dolls and animals. Annie stood near a window watching the rain fall. From a distance, a rider came toward the house. He was covered with an oil cloth to stay dry, so Annie didn't recognize him until he dismounted and uncovered his head as he knocked on the door of Father's office. She recognized the tavern keeper's son.

A moment later, her father opened his office door. The rider held out a letter which he took from an oil cloth bag tied to his waist. Annie saw her father take the letter, nod, and then shut the door. The rider put the oil skin back over his head and strode across the muddy drive to the kitchen.

Not long after, he came out wiping crumbs from his mouth. He gathered his horse from the livery and set off down the road back to Hanover.

She turned from the window back to the children's tea. "I'll have a scone," she said to Elizabeth who had taken over the hostess duties while Annie had been at the window.

"Then you must sit with us, Annie," said Elizabeth. "It's not polite to stand and eat."

Annie pulled a chair up to the table and nibbled at her scone. She looked over at Mary, the nurse, who was in the corner knitting. "Mary, will you have anything?" she asked.

"Not me," Mary answered. "I need to finish this sleeve, and I've only a few rows to go. I only wish the light was better."

"Why not sit closer to the window? Surely there's enough daylight to brighten your work," Annie said.

"But the draft is too chilly. I'm cozy where I am. Let me work a little longer, though."

Annie walked restlessly back to the window. The rain had let up, but there was still no trace of the sun. "Oh I wish I could go outside," she said. "I can't stand being cooped up inside any longer. Hasn't this been the longest February, and the dreariest, that you remember? Even the militia isn't drilling. Father hasn't been to Smith's Tavern for weeks."

"We haven't had a nice spell of sun for weeks, you're right. And we're all about to go stir crazy," Mary answered.

As Annie stood at the window she saw her father stride out of his office, his skull cap pulled down on his head. He walked briskly toward the house, a look of irritation drawing his mouth down at the corners. He entered the back door and called out Patsy's name.

Annie glanced at the children. They were involved in their tea party. Mary was busy. Annie made up her mind to go down and find out what was going on.

Mary looked up at her as she opened the stairway door. "Curiosity killed the cat, little Annie. Spying on other folks won't bring you anything good. If they have something to tell you, they will tell you."

"I'm going anyway," Annie said. She didn't wait for an answer.

It wasn't hard to find her father. His voice carried

throughout the house. "What do you mean you wrote to Cousin Elizabeth Watson? What good could come of it?"

Patsy's response was muffled by her tears. "I only meant to help. I wrote her about John Fontaine . . . and mentioned how poorly Mama's been. I also told her about your activities at the convention. I didn't mean anything by it."

"Well, Elizabeth Watson surely did mean something. She's written a letter." Patrick Henry waved the offending piece of paper. "And she is urging me to send the children to her. She suggests my home is no place for children. I'm too interested in politics, she says, and traitorous politics, she suggests."

Annie fought an urge to rush into the room to defend her father. Instead, she crept closer so that she could hear Patsy's response.

"I never intended for the children to go with her," she said. "But you must think about Annie, Father. The babies I can handle. They don't know what is going on. But Annie is a wild one. She comes and goes as she pleases. She wanders this farm all day long. I can barely get her to study her lessons. She needs some civilizing, and she won't listen to me."

"Well, she won't go to that family," Annie heard her father say. "If something happens to your mother, we'll talk about other arrangements. But I won't hear of it until then."

Annie barely had time to scramble back to the stairs before her father was out the door, slamming it behind him.

Annie's first impulse was to follow him back to his office. She ran out the back door but halted on the stairs. She didn't want her father to be angry with her for eavesdropping. Nor did she want to go back upstairs and listen to more childish chatter. Instead, she ran down the stairs toward the kitchen, grabbed an oilskin that hung on the porch, and tied it around her. A pair of muddy garden boots also sat on the steps. She pulled them on. They were several sizes too big, but Annie didn't care. She darted around the corner of the kitchen, careful to keep out of sight of the windows.

Soon she was in the orchard. The rain had all but stopped, but the slush-covered ground made running close to impossible, and Annie felt out of breath after going only a short way. The month of confinement had made her unused to physical exertion.

She continued walking until she was well out of sight of the house and other outbuildings. Then she tried running some more. Her long skirts, now soaked and splattered with mud, twisted around her legs, nearly tripping her once or twice. When she put her foot down, the snow and slush gripped her boots with such strength that Annie felt she would surely lose them. Ignoring the discomfort, she walked and walked until she was far from

Scotchtown, far from her father, and far from Patsy's plotting.

Annie stayed outside until her anger passed. She walked along a stream that was close to overflowing its banks. Where normally the water trickled, it now raced with thunderous fury. She sat well back from the bank, careful to keep the oilskin under her. She threw branches into the water and watched the creek swallow them up and spit them out far downstream. Once in a while, a branch was caught in an eddy. Water poured down on it, but the hapless twig could only swirl in circles, unable to break the death grip the eddy had on it. Finally, as though an unseen hand had loosed it, the twig would break free and continue on its course.

That's me, Annie thought. Caught in an eddy. One thing after another and I can't get loose of it. She stiffened herself, unwilling to cry. She felt her anger burn towards Patsy. But although Annie tried to nurse her anger, she found it hard to hold on to. After an hour she felt tired, wet and cold—but empty of emotions. I might as well get home, she thought. It's probably lunchtime.

She hopped up but didn't try running back. She didn't have the energy. Instead, she followed the stream as it meandered toward the house.

As she walked, Annie heard the unexpected sound of music. She climbed a little ridge to get a better look. There was a young man, about John's age, playing a flute. He was a lanky fellow, about as tall as Father, and clad in buck-skin. He appeared intent on his music and probably wouldn't have noticed Annie except that her boot slipped on the mud, causing her to fall with a thud.

The young man looked startled. He yelled up at Annie, who was still on the ground, "Who are you? What are you doing here?"

"What do you mean, what am I doing here?" Annie answered back. "This property belongs to my father. You are trespassing. I've a mind to report you." Annie's stern tone was marred by a sudden case of the hiccups.

"Your father," he sputtered. "Not so. My father bought this land from Patrick and Sarah Henry last August. County court just met February 14 to acknowl-edge the sale. The records are there. Go see for yourself."

Annie bit her lip. She knew her father had been sell-ing off parts of the estate. She remembered last August when some local farmers had been called in to witness the deed. Even Mama had been well enough to sign—that had been right before Father had left for Philadelphia.

"Well, I don't care whose property it is," Annie said. "A gentleman wouldn't talk that way to a lady."

The young man blushed red. A quick grin came to his face. "I'm sorry. You actually scared me for a bit. I thought maybe you were a Tory spy—a friend of the king. I shouldn't have spoken so sharply."

Annie's curiosity was quickened. "If I were a Tory spy," she asked, "why would I want to spy on you?"

"Well, 'cause you'd want to know how we patriots are plotting to defend our homes from British tyranny. You'd want to know our plans and see our training exercises. You'd even want names . . . . But I'd never tell. If I ever told a spy the names of some of our leaders—why they could be hung in England, that's what they'd be. Who are you, anyway?"

The young man closed his mouth abruptly as he realized he had been blurting to a stranger. Annie laughed. "I'm Annie Henry. Patrick Henry is my father."

He blushed again. "Pleased to meet you. You must be a patriot then. Your father is a fine man. He's responsible for Hanover County having raised this militia." The boy paused to think, "Have you heard what's happening in Massachusetts? British troops have poured into Boston. The Gazette said fourteen regiments plus Massachusetts Tories have taken over the city. Can you imagine those redcoats trying to take over the Hanover County court-house? We wouldn't let them."

Annie felt a surge of jealousy. Surely Father knew about Boston. But he never talked about it at home. Not something young ladies needed to worry about, he thought—so his daughter had to hear the news from a neighbor boy. Annie nodded as though she knew what the young man was talking about.

The boy was so taken with his own knowledge that he paid scant attention to the young girl's response. "The papers say that Peyton Randolph has called a meeting. Every county is to send two representatives. My pa says your father will be a representative for sure. It's in Richmond next month, on March 20."

"Why Richmond?" Annie asked. "Don't the Burgesses usually meet in Williamsburg?"

"This is different. Governor Dunmore has warships in the York River. If the patriots met in Williamsburg, there might be a fight. Maybe the British would break up the meeting or arrest the leaders. Instead, your father and the others are going to St. John's Church in Richmond. You know, that's not so far from here. I'd give anything to go."

Patrick Henry's daughter thought for a moment about the meeting, but then looked curiously at the boy and his flute. "Why are you playing that, and why are you doing it outside on such a miserable day?" she asked.

"I could ask you the same question," the boy answered. "What are you doing outside on a miserable day?"

"Just walking, but at least I'm not fool enough to be playing music," she said.

"I'm practicing. I'm going to play the fife with the Hanover regulars," the boy said proudly. "I'll be marching with your brother William and your father, if the British don't hang him first."

Annie gasped. "Hang him? Hang Father? They couldn't do that," she said.

"They will if they catch him in a treasonable act; they surely will. And your father is just the man to say something they might take to be disloyal to the king . . . ." The boy paused for a breath. A look at Annie's pale face made him realize how those words sounded. "I'm sorry. That sounded awful. What I meant to say is that Patrick Henry is the finest speaker in Virginia, maybe in all the colonies. Plus, my pa says your father has a passion for liberty. I just figured that those two things might get him into trouble."

Annie remembered suddenly that she had been gone from home too long. She turned to go and hadn't walked more than 100 feet when she realized she didn't know the boy's name. She turned around and yelled, "What's your name, anyway?"

"Andrew Thacker," he called back.

Annie waved. "Andrew Thacker," she whispered to herself. He must be Mrs. Thacker's boy. Annie smiled as she ran toward home. Her boots made a sucking sound as they caught in the mud.

She removed the boots and oilskin at the kitchen and left them on the porch, then carefully made her way across the yard in her bare feet. The wet and grimy hem of her dress rubbed roughly against her ankles.

Trying to sneak into her room so she could change before being seen by Patsy, she walked through the two dining rooms and into her bedroom. As Annie changed, she heard sobs coming from the parlor. She tiptoed to the door, which was slightly ajar. Patsy sat in her mother's favorite chair, head bent, face covered with her hands. She was crying.

Annie felt a sense of dread. Patsy hardly ever cried. She certainly wouldn't be crying over their father's morning anger. No, Annie felt it in her stomach. Something awful had happened.

9

MAMA'S GONE

PATRICK HENRY WASN'T IN THE HOUSE. ANNIE RAN upstairs. She reached the nursery, breathless, with fear in the pit of her stomach. Annie knew as soon as she saw the nurse cuddling Elizabeth that her fears were right.

"Is it Mama?" she asked.

The old nurse, Mary, nodded. She held out her arms to Annie, inviting her to be comforted, but Annie shook her head. She stumbled back down the stairs. By now the tears streamed down her face. Annie ran out the door around to the side of the house to the stairs that led to her mother's room. The door was open.

One female slave carried out old linens as another carried in mysterious bottles with names like myrtle wax, used to anoint the bodies of the dead.

They ignored Annie as they briskly walked back and forth to do their appointed chores. She crept toward her mama's door. It too was ajar. Shutting her eyes, not wanting to see but feeling that she must, she took a deep breath and forced herself to look. There was Sarah Shelton Henry looking more peaceful in death than she had looked in life—at least in Annie's memory. She had already been bathed. The wretched straight dress that had kept her arms bound was nowhere to be seen. Tildy stood near Sarah's head, rubbing some sort of lotion on her. The old slave looked up at Annie with a kind look.

"Your mama's gone, child. She's in heaven now. No more tears for your mama. Don't cry. Your mama's finally found her peace." Then Tildy bent her kerchief-covered head back down to her task.

Annie stood watching for a little longer. Suddenly she wanted to see her father. She left the room and dashed outside across the lawn to his office. But once there she felt timid. She couldn't just barge in. Instead, she knocked softly at the door.

"Come in," her father's voice called out. Annie pushed the door open. She saw him slumped in his rocker, staring into the distance. Wearing the skull cap that he sometimes put on his balding head, Patrick Henry looked much older than his thirty-seven years. He looked up when Annie entered and held out his arms to her.

The rest of that week passed in a blur of activity. Patsy wrote letters to out-of-town family telling them the news. She visited with the many friends and neighbors who came to pay their respects. Annie didn't have any particular job to do. She stood politely and curtsied when addressed. She ran errands for Patsy. She stood at Mama's graveside under the lilac tree. During the years of Mama's illness, that lilac tree had been a comfort to her. Even now, although it was still cold and dreary outside, the lilac swelled with the promise of new life.

Annie took to walking. The rain had ceased and a string of sunny days dried up the mud. She was able to wander far and wide without being missed. Several times she wandered to the stream where she had seen Andrew Thacker, but he wasn't there.

One day, she packed a lunch and set off for a walk. The cloak she wore to ward off the cold wind was short and didn't hinder her from running. Annie ran towards the stream until she could run no longer. Her heart felt bursting in her chest and her throat was raw from the cold air. But she felt good.

She walked until she came to the ridge where she had last seen Andrew. There he was, practicing on his flute. Annie called out, "Hello. How are you, Master Thacker? Mind if I trespass?" she asked with a smile.

He blushed, remembering his words at their last meeting. "Much better weather today," he said.

Annie nodded. She settled herself onto a rock and put the lunch down beside her. "That's true, but a soldier has to march in all kinds of weather. Would you like to share my lunch?"

Andrew grinned. "Ma would tell you not to ask that question. I'm always hungry, and I've never turned down food." He took a seat next to Annie.

Annie took out scones with slices of ham. "I'm sorry, but I brought nothing to drink," she said.

"No matter. The stream is clean. We can drink water," Andrew said as he bit into the biscuit. "I'm sorry about your mother," he said. "I didn't know she was so sick."

She nodded. Annie hadn't cried for days, and she thought she'd like telling Andrew about her mother. "She'd been sick since Edward was born, almost three years. But you know, I always thought she'd get better. I guess I imagined that I'd come home one day and Mama would be sitting in her parlor working on a piece of embroidery like in the old days. I didn't figure she'd die."

"Sometimes death's a mercy, leastwise that's what Pa says," Andrew said. "I guess sometimes life can be so awful that death is the better thing. Do you think that's true?"

Annie tried to remember what she had heard. "Patsy says that Mama fell asleep in the Lord. She says that Mama will be in heaven—and that I might see her one day. Father said that he'd prayed for the Lord to take Mama. I guess he thought death would be a mercy. But you know, it's awful lonely." Annie thought she might cry.

She clenched her teeth and swallowed hard. She did not want Andrew Thacker to see her tears.

As though he could read Annie's mind, Andrew looked down at his food. She quickly wiped a tear from the corner of her eye. Then she said, "I'm probably going to be sent away. Patsy wants to send me to Cousin Elizabeth, but Father says she's a Tory, and he won't have me go. But I heard him talking to Patsy last night. He says I might go to be with Uncle William and Aunt Anne. They're going out west to Fincastle, on the other side of the mountains.

"That's too bad," Andrew said, trying not to gloat. "I get to go to Richmond. Father is going to take a wagon to spring market. We need to buy seed and sell some things. He knows I want to be there, and he said I could go if the chores get done."

Annie swallowed her jealousy and managed to say, "That sounds wonderful, Andrew. I know you're happy."

They finished their lunch in silence, and after a while Annie felt cold. "I'd better get home," she said, "though it is a mighty depressing place to be." She looked hesitantly back in the direction of Scotchtown.

Andrew said quickly, "You come to my house. It's just over the hill. Mama will fix you something hot to drink, and I'll bring you back in the wagon later. How will that be?"

She smiled shyly. "I'd like that. I don't really want to go home quite yet."

The Thacker house was not nearly as grand as Scotchtown. It had only three rooms, not sixteen. It was furnished plainly, in good country style. Mr. Thacker was a farmer—and a good one. He made a comfortable living for his family, but they weren't rich.

Andrew pulled Annie into a kitchen that was nearly as big as half the house. At its center was a huge fireplace and a rough-hewed table that could easily seat ten. Mrs. Thacker looked up from her work and greeted Annie with a laugh and a smile.

"Annie Henry. I'd hoped you'd come visit sometime," Mrs. Thacker said warmly, giving Annie a hug.

Andrew looked at his mother and at Annie. "I didn't know you two knew each other."

"We've met once or twice," Mrs. Thacker said. She brushed her flour-covered hands on her apron. "I could fix you some tea; I still have some I've been hoarding, or I could get you some cider. Which will it be?"

"Cider would be fine, Mrs. Thacker," Annie said.

"Spoken like a true patriot. But we wouldn't expect any less from Patrick Henry's daughter," Mrs. Thacker answered.

Annie swelled with pride. She liked being thought of as a good patriot. Mrs. Thacker heated the cider over the fire. She poured herself a cup and one for Annie, shooed

Andrew out of the room, and pulled a chair up alongside the table.

"Cold day to be outside, isn't it?" she began.

Annie nodded, appreciating the way the cider seemed to burn a path from her throat to her stomach.

"Annie, I'm so sorry about your mother. What a sad thing. And your father with such responsibility."

The young girl hesitated for a minute. She felt drawn to Andrew's mother because the woman reminded her of her own mama. Finally, Annie spoke, "Mrs. Thacker, may I ask you something?"

"Of course you may."

"Why do you think Father travels so much? Mama was so sick, and Father was always going to the Burgesses or to a convention. If he had stayed home, don't you think Mama would have gotten better?"

"Oh, Annie. You can't blame your father for this sickness. He did everything he could do for your mother. It would have been easier to send her away to the asylum, but he didn't do that. And as to why he was away so much, I think you need to understand that your father has great skill as a speaker and lawyer. Virginia needs him now. The people respect him."

"But we need him now," Annie protested and began to weep.

Mrs. Thacker drew Annie close and let her cry. She patted her back and smoothed the hair off her forehead.

Then she said, "Annie, these may seem like hard words. But I want you to listen. You need to guard yourself that no root of bitterness grows up between you and the Lord, or you and your father."

"What do you mean?" Annie asked.

"I mean anger at the Lord because He's taken your mother. And anger at your father because he is trying to serve you and Virginia. God has ordained this moment for your mother to die and a new country to be born. Your father has been called to take part in both events. Think how hard it is for him. Try to help him. Pray for him, but don't be angry with him."

Annie wiped the tears from her face. "I won't be much help to him if he sends me away out west. I don't want to go."

Mrs. Thacker smiled. "I know you'll find a way to help. You are your father's daughter."

Forcing a smile, Annie said, "I guess I'm as stubborn as he is. You're right. I will find a way to help."

Just then, Mrs. Thacker glanced out the window. "My, it will be dark before too long. We must get you home before your father is sick with worry." She opened the door and yelled for Andrew. "Andrew, harness up the wagon. You must take Annie home."

When Andrew came around the house with the wagon, Mrs. Thacker gave Annie a kiss. "Take care, dear. I'll be over to see if I can help Patsy." She turned to her son and said, "Andrew, no dawdling. Annie needs to get home, and you've got chores to do."

She stood and waved as the wagon pulled away.

10

MIDNIGHT RIDE

ANNIE SAT ON THE FRONT LAWN TRYING TO FASHION a crown out of a yellow-blossomed forsythia branch. The branch was too stiff to tie, and every time Annie thought she had it, the branch sprang open in her hand. Finally, she gave up. She cut a few more branches off the bush and thought she'd take them to her father. Annie knew he was busy, and Patsy had told her to leave him be. "He has a lot on his mind," her older sister said. "You need to help him by staying out of his way."

But Annie didn't think he'd mind if she brought him some flowers. She walked over to his office carrying the bouquet in her hand. She peeked in his window and saw him hunched over a Bible. She could tell he was preoccupied. His wig was askew as if he'd been absentmindedly twirling it. He often did when he concentrated.

She decided the flowers could wait. As she wandered

back to the house, a wagon, pulled by the most pathetic horse Annie had ever seen, rolled up the road to Scotchtown. Annie stopped to watch the spectacle. As the wagon drew closer, she saw that it was driven by a women with two little children clinging to her side. The woman's bonnet was dirty, and her dress was wrinkled as if she had slept in it.

Patrick Henry strode out from his office to meet the wagon. Annie watched him speak to the woman, then help her down. He carried the two children, one in each arm, up to the house. Annie followed this unusual parade.

Her father had seated them in the family dining room. He motioned for a servant to bring food and a pot of cider, and sat quietly while they ate. Annie was startled by how quickly they devoured the plate of food set before them. The children ate as if they were starving.

When they had satisfied themselves, they looked up, suddenly aware that the dining room had filled with folks. Patrick Henry, John Fontaine, Annie, Patsy, Elizabeth, and Edward all waited expectantly to hear the strangers speak.

Patrick Henry introduced the woman as Mrs. Beale of Norfolk, Virginia. Then she spoke. "Thank you for taking us in like this. We've been on the road for five days, depending on the kindness of strangers. We're headed west, away from this trouble and madness. I have family there. They'll take us in."

"But where's your husband?" Patsy asked.

Mrs. Beale gave Patsy an odd look. "My husband was taken by British soldiers and their Tory friends. He was tarred and feathered because he wrote newspaper stories defending the colonies and begging the king to relent of his tyranny."

"Tarred and feathered?" Annie asked.

"He was dipped in hot tar and rolled in feathers," she answered abruptly. "He died shortly after from the burns. Now my children are half-orphans, and I must depend on the charity of strangers."

The woman sounded bitter, but she did not cry.

The Henry family looked around uncomfortably. They were surrounded with wealth and comfort. Even though they had suffered their own tragedy, they were not homeless. They were not impoverished.

It was almost more than Annie could bear. "Please let me give your daughters some of my things. I'm nearly ten years old—too old for dolls. Let your girls have them," she begged.

The woman smiled a bitter smile. "They need more than dollies, though I thank you kindly for your generosity. My daughters have been robbed of their future, and you can't give it back to them. I hate this coming war. I hate the king, but I hate the patriots just as much. Why should a good man be taken and his children left fatherless?"

Patrick Henry spoke for the first time. "We grieve with you and hope that you will find comfort in the arms of the Comforter. But Mrs. Beale, you must teach your daughters to be proud of their father. He defended the government of Virginia against the claims of the king and the lords in London who are trying to overthrow our government. I know it is complicated, but your husband's legacy to his children is a proud one. Teach it to them. Teach them to treasure it, not to despise it."

But Mrs. Beale shook her head. Annie understood suddenly what Mrs. Thacker meant by a root of bitterness, and she wanted no part of it.

The Beales stayed for several days at the urging of Patrick Henry. He supplied the girls with new clothes and gave Mrs. Beale some money so that she would not be a burden to her relatives. Annie watched them leave and wondered what would happen to them.

The same day the Beales left, Patrick Henry called Annie and Patsy to his office. They found their father seated at his desk, a letter in his hand. "Sit down," he said. Then, speaking seriously to them, he continued, "Daughters, you know how sorry I am about your mother. I know you miss her. And now I have to be gone as well. I must go to Richmond again, for the convention.

He paused, then continued, "You saw the Beales. You see that there is trouble in the land. There are spies everywhere. Of course it is worse in Norfolk, but we could easily have trouble here. They'd like nothing better than to arrest me. I have to be vigilant, always watching. I can't let myself be distracted with worry about you."

He stopped speaking for a minute, then continued as though the words were almost too difficult to say. "You know I love you, but, Annie, you'll have to go out west to your Aunt Anne's and Uncle William's. In Fincastle, you'll be safe from spies, and I won't have to worry over you."

Annie protested. "Father, let me stay. Please. I won't be a burden. I'll be a help to you."

He smiled sadly. "I'd like you to help in this cause. I've always known you have a faithful, patriot's heart. But you'll be happier at Aunt Anne's."

"I'd be happier with you," Annie insisted. "But I will do what will help you the most."

A look of relief flooded her father's face. Annie realized that he had expected a fight.

"I'm sorry, Annie," he said. "But this will be best." Then he looked down at his work and said, "I must study a little more now."

Patsy went back to the house. But Annie didn't want to be inside. She ran toward the Thacker house.

They were all busy doing farm chores to get ready for their trip to Richmond, but Mrs. Thacker sat on the porch with Annie. She listened sympathetically as Annie complained. "I am going out west. It's all settled. Why must I be so young and a girl? Father isn't sending the boys away."

Mrs. Thacker mused absentmindedly, "You could be a real help to your father—but he knows best, Annie." She looked apologetically at the young girl. "I can't stay and talk. There's too much to do. We have to fill our wagon with harnesses, wool, blankets, and brooms that we made last winter. But, I'll be by to see you before you go away."

Annie shrugged. She walked over to where Andrew was carrying baskets of potatoes to the wagon. "When do you leave?" she asked.

"Day after tomorrow, early. Pa says at first light. We have a lot of marketing to do. When does your father leave?"

"Father leaves then also. He says the convention starts the day after. I wish I were going," she said wistfully. "You will have to save up details to tell me."

"I will," Andrew promised.

At home, Annie kept out of Patsy's way. At night she slept badly. Her sleep was disturbed by dreams of spies and patriots being tarred and feathered. When she awoke in the morning, she felt uneasy. Surely there was a way she could help her father. Didn't she have an obligation to help? Didn't Mrs. Thacker say she'd be a help? Annie pondered these things without knowing what to do.

The next evening, their father played his violin to the gathered family. From the firelight, she could see that his face was drawn and his eyes tired. He was clearly worried. Then he rose and said, "I've a long day ahead of me tomorrow. I'll say 'good-bye' now because I'll not see you in the morning." He hugged each child, and he whispered to Annie, "Be strong and courageous. I will not be gone long."

Annie couldn't sleep. She lay in bed for hours tossing and turning and listening to Patsy's steady breathing. "Lord," she prayed. "Help me to do what's right." Although she knew in her heart she should go west, she couldn't. "Forgive me Lord," she said. "But I must help my father. I must go to Richmond."

She hopped out of bed and pulled on a warm dress, woolen stockings, and her leather boots. She tiptoed to the door. Patsy didn't move. Annie turned the knob slowly and waited. No sound. Then she pulled the door open and glided soundlessly across the wood floors. Once in the dining room, she stood motionless, listening. Again there were no sounds. The outside door squeaked as she opened it. Annie froze. But the house was quiet. She ran down the stairs into the dark night.

Annie knew there were old coats near the kitchen. She slipped across the yard in the moonlight and found a hunter's jacket hanging there. She pulled it on and filled the pockets with apples from a barrel and biscuits, then hitched up her skirts so she could run more easily and started off across the fields.

Annie didn't like the dark. She never had. The tree branches creaked in the wind. Animals made strange sounds, and shadows cast by the moon blanketed the ground in front of her. She shivered, but she was determined to keep going. She knew that she had to reach the Thackers before they set out for Richmond.

Glad that the moon was out and there was some light by which to find her way, she crossed the familiar fields toward the Thacker house. It took more than an hour for Annie to get there, but finally she spotted the wagon in the yard. She laughed with relief and crept silently toward it. All she had to do now was avoid being seen by the Thackers.

Annie looked around carefully and then climbed into the wagon. She burrowed into the hay and piled some brooms and other things on top of her, hoping that she was covered. Then she fell asleep.

The next morning Annie awoke to the rolling and bumping of wagon wheels. The sun was already out, and she could hear Andrew and his father. Annie wanted to climb out from under the hay and join them, but she knew they would take her back home if she did. She figured if she could stay quiet for five hours, they would be too far from home to return.

The hay tickled her nose, and Annie had to keep from sneezing. She felt her stomach rumble from hunger, and she prayed that the growling, which seemed so loud to her ears, could not be heard by the Thackers. Annie nibbled on biscuits that had grown stale and dry. She savored the juice from her apple, trying to let it satisfy her thirst.

For what seemed like hours, she sat quietly in the back, afraid to move or make any noise at all. She didn't know how much time had gone by when she felt something crawling on her leg. Annie froze. The something slithered under her skirt, tickling her leg.

Quickly and quietly she prayed, but the slithering continued. Finally, she could bear it no longer. I can't stand it, she thought as she desperately brushed the hay off her face and tried to dig her way out of the wagon.

Andrew yelled, and Mr. Thacker slowed the horses. He demanded to know the meaning of this, and Annie suddenly felt very foolish.

"There's something under my skirt," Annie said with a shudder.

"Jump over the side," Andrew said. "Shake your skirt."

Annie did as she was told, and a foot long grass snake fell from her petticoats and crawled away.

Annie recoiled. "Yech, I hate snakes," she said, forgetting for a minute that she was in big trouble. Mr. Thacker's stern face recalled that fact to her. She gulped as he stood quietly, waiting for her to explain herself.

"I just had to go to Richmond," she said finally. "I'm to be sent away to Fincastle next week. This is my only chance to be part of my father's struggle. Please let me stay."

Mr. Thacker was silent. Andrew had turned his back to her, but Annie could tell by the movement of his shoulders that he was laughing. Mr. Thacker was slower to relent.

"You haven't left me much choice. We are only a mile from Richmond. We'll find your father, and he'll have to deal with you. You might as well ride on the seat with us," he said.

Andrew pulled Annie up to the wagon seat. He offered her some water and some fresh food from their basket. "How did you get away?" he asked eagerly.

Annie wasn't sure that Mr. Thacker would approve. She knew that Father didn't like disobedience, and this was surely disobedience. She suddenly realized what a terrible thing she had done. She said, "I slipped away and fell asleep in your wagon; and when I woke up, here we were."

A frowning Mr. Thacker replied, "I'd not like it if my daughter ran away and then tried to pretend she hadn't plotted and schemed. I'd rather she confessed boldly and explained why she did it."

Mr. Thacker urged the horses on. He was quiet the rest of the trip, but Annie thought about what he'd said.

11

"GIVE ME LIBERTY OR GIVE ME DEATH"

THE THACKER WAGON WAS NOT THE ONLY ONE rolling toward the market town of Richmond. Many farmers were bringing their produce into town. From Richmond it could travel down the James River to Williamsburg, and from Williamsburg goods traveled across the ocean.

Annie waited with anticipation to see the town. Richmond was still small, but it was bigger than Hanover, which consisted only of the courthouse and the tavern. Richmond did not gleam and glisten, as Annie had imagined, but its main streets were brick and cobblestone, not dirt. Some were lined with row houses, little homes that were hooked together on both sides.

The streets were full of wagons and horses. People

hurried. Instead of tipping their hats and greeting one another, they seemed eager to get on with their business.

Mr. Thacker drove directly to St. John's Church. It was a small, white frame building with a square tower. It sat on a hillside, and the tower was visible for a good distance. Not far from the church was a tavern, and Mr. Thacker walked briskly to the tavern after warning the children to stay in the wagon.

As soon as he was out of earshot, Annie turned to Andrew. "Is your father angry? Does he think I'm awful?" she asked.

Andrew laughed. "I think he figures you have spirit. If the patriots have as much courage, we'll be fine." Then Andrew added reluctantly, "But if it was me who did what you did, I'd be in big trouble—even if I did it for a good cause. Pa says children should obey their parents."

Annie groaned. "My father thinks that also," she said. "But maybe he'll not be angry."

They glanced back in the direction that Mr. Thacker had gone and saw him coming back. With him was an obviously angry Patrick Henry. His wig was flopping. His expression was stern. Annie chewed her lip. Why had she come? she wondered.

Patrick Henry reached the wagon first. "What has gotten into you, young lady?" her father demanded. "Patsy is right. You need training. And Aunt Anne will know how to do it. Obviously my methods have not worked. You are as wild as an Indian, with half as much sense."

Her chin quivered, but he seemed not to notice. He continued, "Did it dawn on you that it isn't safe for a young girl to be out at night? Didn't you know there are animals, even wolves, that would find you a tasty morsel? What about thieves or bandits? Even Tories? Annie Henry, didn't you think about Patsy? What must she be thinking?"

Annie gasped. She honestly hadn't given one thought to how Patsy would feel. Annie had only wanted to come to Richmond. She looked up at her father with dismay. "I'm so sorry, Father," she said. "I only wanted to be with you. I wanted to help. I wanted to be a patriot."

Her father's eyes were still hard with anger, and Annie drew back from him. Then he sighed and turned to Mr. Thacker, "I don't know how to thank you. I'll have to deal with her later."

Thacker nodded. "She's not too big to be spanked," he said pointedly.

Patrick Henry agreed and picked Annie up off the wagon seat. "I love you, daughter. But it wasn't right for you to disobey. I can't send you back now, so you'll have to stay. Let's hope you don't get into trouble."

"I am sorry about Patsy," Annie said.

He nodded. "No matter, we'll send a messenger. Perhaps, I should send you back with the messenger," he said. Annie opened her mouth to protest but thought better of it. Her father shook his head. "No, too dangerous. It's hard to know who to trust anymore. I won't risk it. Now come, and we'll get you situated."

He and Annie walked down the street to a rooming house where Uncle William and Aunt Anne were staying for a week until they returned home to Fincastle. He explained the problem to them while Annie cleaned up. Then he took her out to see Richmond.

There were many men dressed in fancy knee breeches and silks, their hair hidden under powdered wigs. But there were also men dressed in frontier garb who had traveled long distances through muddy roads and spring rains to get to Richmond for the meeting.

"Who are these folks?" Annie asked her father.

"Men here for the convention," he answered. "The fancy ones are the Tidewater planters. They own the big plantations near the Potomac River. The others come from western Virginia—near Anne and William. They've had a hard trip here. Traveling isn't easy in the early spring. But they'll play a role in this convention—you watch."

"How did Mr. Thacker find you so easily?" Annie asked.

"At the tavern. That's where we go to find the news. It hasn't been good, child. There are more stories of patriots being tarred and feathered for what they believe. Two men from Hanover County have been threatened with exile if they don't publicly confess their error in opposing the king."

As Annie listened to the stories, she was glad she had come. She wanted to join Father in the great cause of liberty.

Annie and her father strolled down the sidewalk. Like the Tidewater planters, Patrick Henry was dressed in silks, knee breeches, and a tie-back wig. Annie thought he looked distinguished. His high cheekbones, prominent nose, and often-solemn expression made him look more serious than Annie knew him to be. She figured she liked him best when he played the violin. But this meeting was serious, and her father's party face wasn't in evidence.

They approached a tall, red-headed man walking toward them. He slowed down when he recognized Annie's father. "Hello, Patrick, who is this with you?"

"Good to see you, Thomas. This is my daughter, Annie. Annie, meet Thomas Jefferson, one of my allies in the cause of liberty."

Annie shyly curtsied, then stood back and listened as her father and Mr. Jefferson discussed tomorrow's meeting. Mr. Jefferson tipped his three-corner hat to her and proceeded down the street.

They continued to walk. Her father pointed out Richard Henry Lee and Edmund Pendleton, but their names meant nothing to Annie. Across the street, near the tall churchyard wall, she noted a tall man who had a large crowd around him. "Who is that, Father?" she asked.

"That's George Washington. There's no finer patriot in Virginia. We'll be blessed if he comes on our side, child."

The next day her father left the inn early with her Uncle William. Annie had been sentenced to stay home with Aunt Anne. But to make the sentence sweeter, her father said, "Nothing much will happen the next few days. You stay with Aunt Anne and think about what it means to obey. On the fourth day, you may come to the church."

It was hard to stay in the house for three days, but Annie obeyed. On the fourth morning, the churchyard was filled with spectators who crowded around the windows, which were open to let in the warm spring air. Annie dressed herself hurriedly. "May I go across, Aunt Anne?" she asked.

"Go ahead. But be careful, and watch your manners," Aunt Anne answered. "I don't feel well, but perhaps I'll come over later."

Annie didn't wait. She let out a whoop and dashed out the door and across the street, dodging a passing carriage as she ran. The crowd had grown larger, but she managed to squeeze between people and push her way to a window at the back of the church. Her head came just to the bottom of the window, so she could see in.

She found herself looking into a long, narrow room lined with tall pews. Only the men's heads and shoulders were visible above the wooden boxes. The pews faced toward the window where she stood. The pulpit stood directly in front of the window.

The meeting started slowly. Several men stood up and talked about the good old days and the need to preserve them. But after a while, Patrick Henry rose to speak. He said it was ridiculous to think Virginia could return to the past comforts. Then he offered a resolution—Virginia should set up an army to defend itself.

Immediately the room was in turmoil. Some delegates agreed with him, but others rose to argue against him. They called the resolution rash and reckless. Some said it was rushing into war. Others pleaded for patience. They said in time the trouble would pass and the good old days would return.

After a time, it seemed certain that the resolution would be defeated. Annie's father rose again. He opened the door to his pew and began pacing as he talked. Annie had never seen her father in the courtroom or the House of Burgesses. She stood enthralled, oblivious to her stiff legs and aching back. He spoke softly, shoulders gently slouched, his voice just loud enough to be heard in the church and among those near the windows.

Annie noticed that the men standing near her had drawn close to the window. They no longer talked to each other but were listening attentively as Father spoke. One whispered, "the best speaker this country has," and Annie knew they meant her father.

Patrick Henry spoke like a preacher. He stood slightly bent and said, "War is inevitable—and let it come!" A gasp went up from the crowd at the windows. But no one called it "treason."

By now, his voice was louder. He no longer slouched but stood erect so that he looked even taller than his six feet.

"Gentlemen may cry, 'Peace, peace,'—but there is no peace." Then he added, "The war is actually begun . . . . Our brethren are already in the field! Why stand we here idle? . . . Is life so dear, or peace so sweet, as to be purchased at the price of chains and slavery?"

When he said those words, he crossed his arms in front of him as though they were shackled. He paused, then looked up to heaven and said, "Forbid it, Almighty God!" Then, still standing as though in chains, he looked over at the timid Loyalists and said, "I know not what course others may take." Stretching to his full height he proclaimed, "but as for me, give me liberty or give me death!" At the word "death" he moved as if plunging a dagger into his breast.

Annie had been so taken up with the speech that when she saw the hand plunging with the dagger she let out a muffled cry. She stood for a moment in confusion.

The man next to her exclaimed, "When I die, I want to be buried at this spot."

All around, the people talked. She felt she had to get away to breathe. As she moved from the window, she saw a familiar person also leaving the building. He had an angry look on his face. Annie wondered where she had seen him before. Then she remembered. Francis Doyle! The man who had called Father a traitor. He had vowed to stop her father that night at Scotchtown many months ago.

She felt a quick stab of fear as she saw Francis Doyle hurry away. What if he reported Father's speech to the royal authorities? Could that be treason? Could her father be tarred and feathered, or worse yet, hanged? Annie didn't know what to do, so she followed Mr. Doyle as he briskly walked down the street. She had to trot to keep up with his long strides.

So intent on her task was Annie that she did not pay much attention to where they were going. Before long, though, she realized they were headed for the James River. Annie thought she knew Mr. Doyle's plan. He would take a boat down the James River to Williamsburg where the Royal Governor was.

Annie didn't wait to follow. She ran as fast as she could to the wharf. There she found a busy river with merchant ships and fishing boats lining the dock. She glanced over her shoulder and sighed. Mr. Doyle was still a block away. Annie didn't have a plan, but she knew she had to do something.

A man unloading a load of oysters on the dock, turned to her and said in a reassuring Scots accent, "Can I help you, miss?"

She answered, "I'm Annie Henry, Patrick Henry's daughter . . . ." She waited for his reaction.

"A fine man, that Henry," the oyster man said with a broad grin. "If you be his daughter, you are much blessed, because they don't come any finer."

She grinned. "I know that. There's a problem that maybe you could help me with. Do you see that gentleman over there?" and Annie pointed to Mr. Doyle who had just reached the dock. "He's a Tory. He doesn't approve of my father at all and called him a traitor. And he's just heard my father say that war is inevitable." She repeated the lines still ringing in her head. "He said, 'Give me liberty or give me death.'" She waited for a reaction and wasn't disappointed.

"Yes, that's the attitude we must all have," the oyster man said. "No more waiting around for things to get better. They've already gone too far."

Annie interrupted. "I'm afraid Mr. Doyle might be looking for a boat to Williamsburg. He wants to report my father. Maybe he'll try to disrupt the convention. Maybe he'll have my father arrested. What can we do?"

The oyster man thought for a minute. Then he smiled

broadly, "Don't worry yourself. He'll not find a boat today from this dock. I can guarantee it. We're all patriots here. Wait for me. I'll be back soon."

Annie watched as the oyster man walked from boat to boat whispering in the ears of the fishermen. She saw them glance toward Francis Doyle and nod, a look of determination on their faces.

Finally, he came to a boat at the end of the dock. Annie noticed with dismay that Mr. Doyle had already climbed aboard and was sitting on a barrel, clearly impatient to be off. The oyster man called to the boat's captain who came over to listen. Annie saw him nod. He chewed his pipe stem and nodded some more. They shook hands.

Soon, the oyster man returned to Annie. "It's taken care of, dear. He'll not get to Williamsburg, leastwise not soon."

Annie pointed at the boat which held Mr. Doyle. "But they're untying the boat, and Mr. Doyle's still on board," she protested.

"Yes, they will sail out of sight of Richmond, but the captain will make sure they have boat trouble. He's promised they'll be delayed. Probably not get to Williamsburg for a few days. That happens with boats sometimes," he said with a chuckle.

Annie laughed. "Boat trouble. That's funny. Poor Mr. Doyle."

The oyster man laughed also. "Now let me get you back to your father. This isn't the place for a young lady."

Annie nodded gratefully. She realized that she had no idea where she was. She took one last glance at Francis Doyle on the boat, aptly name "The Patriot," sailing slowly out into the center of the James River. "Good-bye, Mr. Doyle," she called out quietly.

Up and down the docks the story spread until Annie was surrounded by fishermen eager to meet her and pay their respects to the daughter of Patrick Henry.

The oyster man finally broke away from the crowd. "We must get this lass home," he said to the other boatmen. "Her father will be worried." They took a wagon back to the rooming house. The oyster man touched the brim of his hat and said, "Tell your father that you are a brave little patriot, and that Capt. James Boyd of Edinburgh, Scotland, is proud to have helped."

Annie waved before heading up the walk to the house. Several hours later Patrick Henry bounded up the steps. "Huzzah, Huzzah," he called as he stooped to hug her. "You are the talk of the town, Annie Henry. Everyone has heard the story of how a brave, little patriot girl foiled the plans of the wicked Tory. I heard it from the fellow selling apples on the street corner. He didn't even know who I was." Her father's eyes twinkled as he swung her around. "I only wish I had my violin so we could celebrate properly."

"May I stay with you at Scotchtown?" Annie blurted out.

Patrick Henry laughed, "You don't give up, do you?" Then he looked pensive, "It will be hard, Annie . . . but what's important is what helps the cause of liberty." He smiled. "You have spirit, Annie Henry, and I love you. Your Aunt Anne's loss is the revolution's gain—and mine. Let's go home."

AUTHOR'S NOTE

ANNIE HENRY AND THE SECRET MISSION IS FICTION. However, there was a real Annie Henry who lived in Virginia with her father, Patrick Henry, brothers, and sisters. Her mother, Sarah Henry, died in early 1775 after a long period of mental illness. Scotchtown and St. John's Church are real places that you can still visit today.

The book is also faithful to the general history of the colonial period. People ate the kinds of food mentioned. They wore the types of clothes described. They performed chores such as fire fighting and harvesting in the manner described in the book.

Patrick Henry played a crucial role in the American Revolution. Whenever possible I have tried to use his own words so that you can get a true idea of what he believed about slavery, war, and liberty. His "give me liberty or give me death" speech put Virginia firmly on the side of independence. The description of that speech comes from eyewitness accounts.

Many people do not know that Patrick Henry was a strong Christian. He wrote about the Bible: "This book is worth all the books that ever were printed."

NOTE

To learn more about Annie Henry
and the revolutionary war, ask for Book 2
in the **Adventures of the American Revolution** series
at your local Christian bookstore.